4op

CW005516862

FOREST HERITAGE

Forest Heritage

MARY WILLIAMS

WILLIAM KIMBER · LONDON

First published in 1986 by
WILLIAM KIMBER & CO. LIMITED
100 Jermyn Street, London SW1Y 6EE

Typeset by Scarborough Typesetting Services
and printed in Great Britain by
Biddles Limited, Guildford and King's Lynn

*For friends
of long ago*

Author's Note

Readers of this book who know the forest area of central England well may identify fictitious hamlets, towns and landmarks with real places. Bradgate Park exists. Other names and places have been altered and contrived to suit the story. All the characters are entirely fictitious.

M.W.

1

She couldn't rest. Watchful and tense, her nerves were stretched almost to breaking point. The ominous approach of thunder looming over the Burnwood hills didn't help. Storms there were violent, as though the ancient heart of the range was erupting to vengeful life again, after countless millions of centuries.

Emma Fairley, born in the vicinity and now in her twentieth year, had become sensitized to every mood of that particular north-western corner of Leyfordshire. Something of its lush sweetness, veiled mystery of its valleys and rugged freedom of rocky summits was in her very blood. A haunted area — one of volcanic origin, which at times could stir the imagination from dreamy peacefulness to a primitive awareness of a far-off bygone age. Apprehension then shuddered through Feyland Woods from the lonely tip of Hawkswycke Hill. The forest wilderness of larch, silver birch, and ancient oaks became a place of shadowed mystery; in the creeping mists of early summer and autumn, twisted branches of sloe and elder were grasping arms — the deep green tarns of Feyland, waiting graves for the unwary.

Emma, on that far off autumn evening, was keyed-up to face not only nature's elemental challenge, but a personal crisis which involved the whole of her future and that of her father, William Fairley —especially the latter. So much was at stake; on his meeting that day with Jonathan Bradley — business tycoon and owner of the new *Leyford Comet*, a daily newspaper intended to oust the well-established *Leyford Courier* — depended the survival of *The Charwood Echo*, her father's own newspaper and particular baby. Bradley was determined to acquire it by fair means or foul. He had the wealth and the power. Already the *Echo* had been hit by the new sensational publication *Comet* which was cheap in price, flashy perhaps, but sufficiently colourful to woo a considerable public!

At the expense of the *Echo*.

And this was only the beginning.

Ultimately?

Emma, who'd been her father's trusted confidante since her mother's death two years previously, shuddered to think. The only real hope, she well knew, was that Bradley might be induced to take up certain shares for a minimum of power on the *Echo*, leaving William and his co-director, Frank Page, in major control.

It was for this that Fairley had gone to Eastwood Hall that day for his meeting with Bradley. Although she hoped desperately for his success, she doubted it; and as the sullen sky darkened towards evening, bringing the first clap of thunder from the hills, her body stiffened, and despondency intensified.

William should have been back an hour — even two hours — ago. Had he called at the office in Charbrook before fortifying himself to bring news to her? Or could there have been an accident? The forest lanes were twisting and narrow, and could be dangerous to transport in the damp fading light, especially in the new-fangled motor car, which her father had insisted on purchasing for daily, quicker transport from home to his newspaper offices at Charbrook. The trap he'd used before was still retained in the stables at Oaklands, with their beloved mare, Lady, and so far the motor car, a Mercedes-Simplex, had not proved worth its cost. Emma herself had already learned to drive it. It could be fun, but not half so much enjoyment as a ride on Lady, and the mechanics worried her. It was the mechanics she feared every time her father set off at the wheel, making such a grinding noisy start to any journey.

She'd wanted him to go on horseback or take the trap that day. Eastwood Hall, as the crow flies, was only fifteen miles away, and on Lady he could have taken short cuts across the country. But William on this occasion had been determined to appear modern and as affluent as possible, setting out at the wheel wearing a sporting check cap and tweed jacket over knickerbockers of the same tone.

'The millionaire look,' he'd told his daughter whimsically, with a little tug of his carefully trimmed Imperial beard. 'I've met the man only twice, but he's a climber. The type always appreciative of style.'

'And money. Mean, I expect,' Emma had retorted shrewdly.

He'd smiled, trying to hide underlying anxiety.

'Don't be cynical, Emma, that's not your type.'

'What do you mean − *my* type?'

He flung her a shrewd glance.

'You know very well. Feminine. Womanly.'

'You sound so stuffy.'

'I am, my dear, over those I care about.'

This was true. But in Emma he recognised very well, there was a quality of excitement and adventure that put her apart— ahead of her time. Not traditionally a beauty, perhaps, but arresting and unpredictable, unlike her mother Claire, whose gentle serenity and fair classical features had provided always a refuge of peace when he needed assurance to steer him through financial and other problems of the *Echo*.

There was nothing really serene about Emma. Beneath her fine-boned, rather delicate exterior, was a quick-silver mind, forever darting this way and that to meet any challenge that might arise. The innocence of her widely-set luminous grey eyes was belied by a provocative tilted mouth in a heart-shaped face; her pert nose was slightly upturned, denoting what he termed a rare capacity for delving and digging into other people's affairs. The small determined chin had a cleft in it, and her head was proudly set on a slender neck.

Yes. Emma was indeed quite a force in his life.

Claire's death in giving birth to Rosalind, a younger daughter, following a dangerous lapse of fifteen years had eventually turned William's affections all the more fiercely on his elder child. He hadn't particularly wanted the new baby, and when she was proved to be backward and incapable of learning to speak or communicate properly, loss of Claire had turned to an inner resentment that could only be overcome by a quiet, almost fanatical determination to keep the family newspaper going — run in the traditional decent way first established by his grandfather.

The *Echo* and Emma.

Being a dedicated clear-sighted man, he recognised that a certain modernisation might be necessary. With moderate expenditure this could be done. But the policy of fair comment must remain. The *Echo* had never been a political publication, and he was determined at this time, following the ending of the Boer War, that he'd restrain it from being influenced too obviously by right or left. All the same — the tempo of life was changing. Liberalism was gaining steadily, and he had a shrewd idea that in a couple of years' time Campbell Bannerman might emerge as Prime Minister. The voice of radicalism was stirring among the minds of the people. Women, too, were showing a desire to play a part in the country's affairs other than mere domesticity. He couldn't see they'd have much success. But the future was chancy and unknowable. Meanwhile let the feminine appeal of the *Echo* have full play. Emma had been a great asset during the past twelve months contributing a weekly column dealing with dress, cooking, and social and gardening observations that for a time had sent the circulation up — a swing of the pendulum that might have continued, but for the sudden appearance on the scene of the *Leyford Comet*. Racy, witty, a little cheap and Americanised, it had gained immediate response.

And Bradley was certainly not going to allow it to decline.

William did not fear for the future of the *Weekly Echo* but the daily publication was a different matter. It was the *Daily* he feared for.

And so did Emma.

Why could life be so unfair and complicated, she wondered, as she wandered time after time to the gate of their garden overlooking the forest? Why must that rich stranger from up country have arrived at such a crucial time to upset things? Why had he to fling his wealth about so vulgarly, just to destroy the even tempo of the *Echo*'s progress, with his power? Her own column week by week had been gathering the interest of new readers. In time (though she hadn't yet broached the suggestion to William) she might even be a regular contributor to the *Daily*. Women journalists were few and far between. But there was no reason on earth why she shouldn't be among the first. Fame didn't particularly appeal to her. But proving herself did — proving that she could be an important factor in helping retain the standards of the respected newspaper established by her forbears so many years ago.

Oh dear! *Why* was he so late?

The housekeeper who'd been with them through and since her mother's illness came down the path, saying irritably, 'Can't you come in now? It's getting damp. And you with nothing on your shoulders.'

Emma smoothed a strand of russet hair from her brow.

'I'm not cold. I like the air.'

'Well, I don't. And it's already spitting with rain. You can't do any good standing about getting wet.'

Emma sighed. 'No. That's true. Very well — go along, Mrs Cox. I'll be there in a moment.'

She was turning to follow the receding figure when the familiar rattling sound of an engine chugged in fits and starts from a bend in the lane. Emma felt a surge of relief, and ignoring the heavy spatter of increasing rain, ran towards the blurred shape of the approaching vehicle. The gates below the house leading to the shed where the car was kept were already open. William turned in awkwardly.

'You're so *late*,' Emma exclaimed. 'I was wondering if you'd overturned into a ditch or something.'

Clambering out, William answered, pulling his cap off and wiping his forehead free of damp, 'You should control that imagination of yours better. There was a puncture about five miles back and I had to change a wheel.'

'Oh. Poor you. What a nuisance. Are you wet?'

'Yes.'

'And what happened? Did he — did you have any success with Bradley?'

'I'll tell you when we get into the house,' William said rather abruptly. '*Please*, my dear. I've had a long day.'

Emma's heart sank. Obviously he had nothing good to report.

Her deductions were correct.

When William had changed and gone into his study for a drink before the meal, he said heavily, 'It's no good, Emma. He won't co-operate. The *Echo* — yes. He wants it, and will invest a tidy sum provided he has an overall majority in the shareholdings. This would mean giving him complete power to alter the character of the paper in any way he chose — so—' he shrugged and gave an expressive gesture of the hands, 'it's no go.'

'But — didn't you *explain* properly? Couldn't he see that although his type of publication might draw in a new public, the present readers like it as it is—'

'Of course I did. But he's a hard thinker, looking ahead to the future. He even has a plan eventually to contain the whole lot — the *Courier*, *Echo* and *Comet* into one paper — *The Midlander*. Oh, he's got his head screwed on pretty firmly, but for once he won't get his way that easily. I'll spike his guns, by God.'

Emma shook her head slowly. How could he? When their annual income was only just sufficient to keep them and the *Echo*, out of debt? 'What plan have you?' she asked. 'If you haven't the money—'

'I *could* have,' he interrupted. 'There's a way. You won't like it. But — I've decided.'

The strained lines of his face — the hard look of hopeless defiance and determination about his mouth and eyes frightened her.

'Tell me.'

'I can sell Oaklands,' he stated, not looking at her. 'It's a unique place and would fetch a good sum. Whoever bought it *might* allow us to remain on a rental basis. It's the only way, Emma.'

'You can't *mean* it. *Oaklands!* It's been in the family for — for

generations. My great-grandfather designed it. It's a heritage –
a duty; an obligation.'

'The *Echo* comes first.'

'But why? *Why?*'

'Tradition – it's the only decent newspaper Charbook's ever
had. And there are other places where we could live.'

Emma could feel her nails biting into the palms of both
hands.

'Not like this,' she said fiercely. 'There's nowhere in
Burnwood to compare. You've said yourself it's unique. Where
else could anyone find a house built from the rock face? It's
listed in books – a feature of the forest—' Emotion half choked
her, bringing the flood of words to a halt.

'I know, my dear. I know—' he slumped forward suddenly,
with his head in his hands. When he glanced up again the
strange greyness of his face temporarily drove all other thoughts
but anxiety from her mind. 'Are you all right, father?' she
queried sharply.

He forced a smile. 'I will be. Pour me another brandy, child.
Oh—' A hand suddenly went to the left side of his chest.

'What is it? What's the matter?'

'Nothing. A touch of indigestion. I get it occasionally when
I'm tired. It'll soon pass.'

'Then you must see a doctor,' she said firmly. 'You've been
working too hard for too long. And all this worry—'

He waved a hand in negation. 'I want no doctor. Fussy old
pessimists all of them. Now, Emma—' He got up, straightened
himself, thumped his chest, and with forced energy said,
'There's life in the old dog yet. So stop worrying. Things will
work out. Just drop the talking now, and in the morning, maybe
we'll both feel differently about things. The pendulum could
swing either way.'

But Emma knew that business pendulums didn't swing that
easily in her father's direction. Especially concerning the *Echo*.

For a moment she almost hated the paper. Hated it for sap-
ping her father's energy, and endangering what were the roots
of their very existence – Oaklands.

That evening, when William had retired to bed, she went downstairs and out into the steamy autumn night.

The thunder had cleared, leaving a freshness of the air, with a pale watery moon filtering through the haze of dying cloud.

Like sentinels of the past, the massed trees of the forest stood dimly shadowed beyond the garden. On one side the tip of Hawkshill was visible momentarily, then faded again. The distant glimmer of Marten Pool shone silver for a second beyond Feyland. An owl called softly from the woods. All was mystery — a threadwork of winding lanes and small lost hamlets. Yet she knew them, had walked them all, climbed every tumpy rock-tipped hill, since childhood. It was her birthright. They couldn't lose it now — neither she nor her father. Somehow both Oaklands and the *Echo* had to be saved.

But how?

Had her father been sufficiently tactful during the meeting with Bradley? When reason failed had he thrown his cards too bluntly on the table? William Fairley, though inherently and by practice diplomatic, could be amazingly defiant when pressed. Perhaps in the end when he'd found the other man so unco-operative he'd let his temper get the better of him and he'd issued a challenge he could not possibly win.

There was, then, only one course left. Without telling her father she'd herself visit Eastwood Hall that Thursday, which was publishing day for the *Echo*, knowing William would be fully occupied at Charbrook and would not miss her. She'd ride Lady cross-country, and deal with the hateful stranger in her own way. What that way would be, she hadn't a clue. Until they met face to face, she'd no way of assessing their instinctive reactions to each other. But she'd dress carefully and suitably, and while keeping her business senses alert, would make the most of her feminine attributes.

When the day arrived, luckily it was fine. She set off early before the silver mist had lifted from the short turf and under-growth. Many of the trees were bare now of foliage, but a few leaves still hung from lean black branches, diamonded with glittering cobwebbed filaments of dew. Much of the forest appeared half-dream, half-reality. As Lady sniffed the air appreciatively passing the old Priory of Uldene, Emma recalled days of her childhood when she'd imagined herself a lost princess in a fairy tale. So much of her was bound up in this area of ancient territory — so evocative a sense of history and days gone by. The lake surrounded by the grouped tall trees, Hawkwycke Hill with its rugged peak and broken prehistoric circle, the deep green slate pits lurking mysteriously between shadowed trunks of oak and birch, and in springtime the acres of bluebells more softly bright than a cloudless summer sky. The ruined priory itself, and the monastery Coldale way where the silent brotherhood worked and had their being. This was enchanted country. Hers and William's. In its way a lost land, because few tourists came there unless it was to visit Bradgate Park and the ruin which had once been the home of Lady Jane Grey, the ill-fated nine-day queen — oh she'd never let Bradley force them away. Never, *never*.

Bringing herself harshly back to reality again she'd kicked Lady to a swift canter, and moments later Uldene had faded into a spectral shape soon completely lost in the shadows of the woods.

She avoided the outskirts of Charbrook, taking footpaths and bridle ways to the opposite side of the county where foxhunting was the chief sport on which the rich spent winter months during the season.

Here the land was more flat and verdant, dotted at intervals with picturesque villages and small market towns. To Emma the landscape, though pleasant, was ordinary. And any appreciation she had for it was marred by her hatred of a sport she considered as barbaric as cock-fighting. Although William, of a necessity, had to show impartiality towards differing sections of the Leyfordshire community, Emma, except for rare social occasions, had kept herself aloof from the snob set — her private term.

Now she had to face that however distasteful it was, she must play the odious 'pretend game' of being appreciative of the wealth, social status, and power of the formidable Bradleys.

Not that the rich Northerner could yet have been genuinely accepted by the county aristocracy. He had lived only two years at Eastwood, and had amassed his fortune from *Trade*. But in time a wily millionaire of his calibre might wheedle a baronetcy from the 'powers-that-be' — provided he paid enough. This would eventually woo him an avowed place in the Burnwood circle.

The whole situation filled Emma with contempt. But the day was fresh and invigorating; the keen sweet wind — redolent with the scents of damp earth, tumbled leaves and blackberries — brought a challenging glow to her cheeks. She rode side-saddle, wearing an olive green velvet habit, with her gleaming dark hair pinned up in a chignon under her tilted boat-shaped hat. A stray curl brushed one cheek, giving extra allure to her feminine elegance. It would have been more fun riding astride, as she frequently did, through the forest, but of course quite outrageous on this occasion. As the silver sun rose higher in the pale sky she felt resentful for a brief moment or two that she hadn't been free to look for mushrooms instead of gallivanting across lush parklands to Eastwood. A quantity of silvered umbrella shaped pale heads had appeared in Starvecrow field on the edge of the Woods when she passed. Tomorrow they would probably be gone, and her father liked them fried on toast. But there was no point in brooding. She kicked Lady to a smart gallop, and reached Eastwood shortly before eleven, wondering how she'd be greeted, and if Bradley's wife ruled there, as some chatelaine or queen.

Well, she'd soon find out.

She dismounted and was about to lead Lady by the bridle down a drive at the side of the mansion, when a man, obviously a groom, wearing gaiters and a leather jerkin over a woollen jersey, appeared from the opposite direction. He was a burly figure, shrewd-eyed, with a crop of ginger hair above a broad pink face. 'Can I help you, ma'am?' he asked. 'Wanting anyone, are you?'

'Mr Bradley,' Emma answered. 'Perhaps you can inform a servant of my arrival.'

'I can take thy horse for a while, but the master isn't in. Is he expecting you?'

The direct question took her aback, but only for a moment.

'He may well be,' she answered coolly. 'My name is Fairley, Miss Emma Fairley. My father was here yesterday.'

'Oh. You mean the newspaper man?'

She nodded.

'Well ma'am — miss, he isn't in. I'm sorry but there it is. Went off ridin' 'bout an hour ago. Whether it's worth thee waitin' a bit—' His Yorkshire voice broke off as a younger, taller man walked smartly through a gate in the drive leading from a field. He must have been well over six feet, and as he drew near Emma felt a stab of surprise — almost shock — seeing how very handsome he was — fair hair licked to brightest gold in the early sunlight, fine-featured, and with eyes so blue they startled her. He was attired fashionably in fawn twill knee breeches and a smartly cut velvet jacket. A silk scarf was knotted loosely, in the manner of a cravat, at his neck. He had a winning smile, slightly tilted to one side, which added to his charm. Obviously a ladykiller, Emma decided after the first impact was over, and one used to getting his way.

She drew herself up an inch or two higher whilst formal introductions were made. Then, when her business was made clear, he said, still with his magnetic gaze fixed upon her, 'Father's out, as you've just heard — unfortunate for you perhaps, but damned lucky for me.'

She flushed faintly.

'I ought to have made an appointment, of course, but—'

'Nonsense. I'm glad you didn't. He shouldn't be long. You can wait, I suppose? This business you have with him is important?'

She nodded decisively. 'Very.'

'Concerning the local rags. Am I right?'

'Yes. Mr — Bradley. You did say "father", didn't you?'

He grinned. 'Oh indisputably. I'm Arthur — the one-and-only. Except for Jessie, of course, my sister. But I'm afraid my rich tycoon of a sire *does* rather concentrate on the importance of having a male heir — however unsatisfactory a one I may be.'

Unable to decide how much of the statement was made in jest, how much in truth, Emma ignored it, and after a brief look round an ornamental garden at the side of the house, which included a pool overhung by willows and a Japanese maple, they went inside.

The interior was as massive as the outward facade of the Hall suggested; the corridors were wide, the rooms large with high encrusted ceilings. The furnishing was rich but unimaginative, comprising a good deal of red plush, gilt, and crystal. Ornate glass-faced clocks, probably French, ticked from marble mantel shelves and alcoves. The drapes were heavy, and the air was over-heated. From a reception room on the left into which Emma was shown, a conservatory led through a glass door to a path bordering a shrubbery. The smell of ferns was strong and heady. Emma had an urge to rush round pushing every possible window open; she felt smothered, sensing that she had come on a fool's errand. Anyone living in such a cloying overpowering atmosphere of ostentatious wealth could not possibly appreciate the wild sweet freshness of Burnwood, or her mission to save Oaklands. The rigidity of her pose, her air of bewildered distaste, didn't escape the young man's attention.

'A bit stuffy,' he commented, 'I agree. But my mother likes warmth, and the pater's not here often. Sit down, though. The chairs are comfortable. Like a drink?'

Emma took the nearest chair which was divided into three back to back, forming a circular design. The seats were low, of rich maroon shaded velvet, and surprisingly comfortable.

'No thank you,' she said primly, refusing the Madeira.

His fine arched brows shot up. 'No? Ah. I forgot. You're here on business.' The mocking note had returned to his voice.

Emma stiffened again.

'Do you mind telling me — I mean, have you any idea how long Mr Bradley will be?'

He shook his head. 'No, I'm afraid not. But I hope it will be a considerable time. Long enough for us to get to know each other.' Her grey eyes met his squarely, and once more she was impressed by their brilliance. He really was astonishingly good-looking; charming too, in his way, although something about him, a secret assessing quality, mildly intimidated her. Quite obviously he found her fascinating. At odd moments his gaze slid appreciatively over the slender lines in her figure, then back to the provocative features under the perky boat-shaped hat, and dark rich gleam of russet hair. A beauty, begad, he was thinking, and quite a character — one well worthy of adding to his retinue of female admirers. Could one have fun with her? Possibly. But it might be a dangerous game, and if Arthur Bradley considered any woman worth dallying with, he expected his own brand of response. Pride alone demanded it. Could he win this one? After a few speculative moments he decided to take up the challenge, and by the time Jonathan Bradley appeared an hour later, he'd succeeded in at least warming her interest.

Jonathan was shorter in height than his son — broader, of burly build, with a square high-coloured face, and determined chin. His eyes were shrewd and fiery below thick brows, lit by sparks of vitality suggesting a hot temper and considerable physical strength. Beneath his well-cultivated voice the north country accent was still strong. In age Emma judged him to be somewhere in the late forties. He was, actually, forty-seven, and Arthur, his son, twenty-five.

Introductions were cordial but brief. During his first few words, following Arthur's departure, Emma sensed she had no more chance than her father of success in her mission, although his appraising glance at the exotic spirited young creature confronting him was appreciative, even a little warm.

'I'm glad to meet you, young lady,' he said, 'relax now and be at ease. Maybe a Madeira would help, eh?' He fetched a decanter and glasses from the cupboard.

'Oh no, thank you,' Emma protested, 'your son *did* ask me, but—'

'Arthur?' Jonathan laughed shortly. 'This is *my* house, Miss Fairley, and if I've a mind for you and me to get down to business in a cosy way, I don't think you'll object. Come now.' He was pouring the wine. 'You've already mentioned business, so shall we start?' As she mutely accepted the glass, he added, 'I can guess what it's about, of course. The *Echo*.'

'Yes.' Her voice and manner were defiant. She had meant to be so tactful and subtle in her approach, but his bluntness, air of command and obvious assumption that he held all the cards before any discussion was begun, stirred her to reckless honesty.

'I don't expect concessions from you,' she said, 'I haven't come to beg or plead with you—'

'Good.'

'I just think if you could see another's — my father's — point of view, without prejudice,' she continued quickly, 'it could be to the advantage of both.'

He regarded her thoughtfully during a short pause, while a tinge of amusement touched his hard mouth. 'And what makes you think that?'

Her colour deepened to a becoming rose. 'Because I've lived all my life near Charbrook. I've grown up knowing of the newspaper's problems, I know what the public want. It's a — well, in a way, a *family* publication. People look for personal tit-bits and gossip as well as more general news. It could have a wider circulation of course, but with money invested this could be easy. Don't you *see*, Mr Bradley, to change its character could be a great mistake? Almost a disaster—' Her voice had changed, softened. The luminous brilliance of her grey eyes affected him in a way he was quite unprepared for.

'Miss Fairley,' he said more quietly, 'I understand your reasons for coming here. You're echoing very much what your father said. *He* knows, as you must, that I'm quite willing to sink a good deal into what is after all — a very minor provincial daily. But it must be on my terms, girl. I'm a businessman. D'you think for one moment I made all the brass I've got from old-fashioned dreams?'

'I—'

He raised a hand. 'No. Hear me out. I can understand your loyalty to Fairley. He's been a good man in his day, but—'

'What do you mean *in his day*? My father's still an active, intelligent editor. And popular—'

'Maybe, maybe. But he needs help, new ideas to face the challenge of the future. And I can give it. Another thing — you could brighten your own little ladies' columns up a bit — get around more, mix with the right set. Your job's safe if you go along with me. You c'n write. I could make you into something — something better than a scribbler on birds and trees. Now think about it. I've given a time limit to all of us. Use it and get facts square.'

'Meaning give you the over-all power? Fifty-one per cent of the shares in the *Echo*?'

'That's right. And believe me you'll find it'll not be half as bad as you think. Fairley will still hold the reins in the office. I shan't interfere except to expand a bit when necessary.'

'But it won't be *his* paper.' Her manner was mutinous.

'Not entirely. He can't afford it, can he?'

She winced, then got up and walking towards the door, said coldly, 'I can see I've wasted my time.'

'Not at all. Best for all of us to have things straight. We'll be meeting again, I've no doubt.'

She was passing through into the hall when a plump yellow-haired woman appeared from a room on the opposite side. She was made up rather badly, with over-rouged cheeks, and was attired fussily in pink; her smile was forced, a little tremulous. A distinct odour of perfume and alcohol tinged the air as she approached.

'Oh!' she gasped, with one small plump beringed hand at her breast, 'I'm sorry, I really am. I didn't know thee had company, Jonathan.' She teetered slightly on her feet.

Bradley frowned. 'My wife, Miss Fairley,' he said.

'Really? I'm delighted.' The broad face smiled, and Emma realised in one quick moment that when young she must have been pretty. Her eyes, half hidden now by puffed lids, gleamed china-blue. Obviously the son, Arthur, had inherited her colouring and one-time good looks. She was trying hard — painfully almost — to be welcoming and lady-like. Her feigned mimicry of the well-bred county accent was not only farcical, but pathetic. It was quite clear to Emma that she was in awe and a little frightened of her husband who was doubtless a bully in his domestic as well as business life.

Emma smiled encouragingly. 'I'm pleased to meet you,' she said.

'You must come over for tea one day,' the older woman said, more naturally. 'Our cook, Mrs Maggs, is a dab hand at cream cakes. Well — in Yorkshire we pride ourselves on our cooking, thee knows — *you* know,' she corrected herself quickly.

'Now, Amelia,' Bradley interrupted warningly, looking for an instant quite furious, 'Miss Fairley didn't come for a lecture on cookery.'

His wife's brief spell of vitality died out of her suddenly, like air from a pricked balloon.

'No, no, Jonathan. Well then — bye bye, luv — Miss Fairley.'

She turned, and with a rustle of silks disappeared like an immense ruffled pouter pigeon into the rosy glow of what was obviously a drawing room.

Minutes later Emma had extricated herself from the unsuccessful encounter with Jonathan, and was cantering on Lady down the drive to the lane. She had just turned the corner when another rider, Arthur Bradley, approached her at a smart pace. He reined alongside, showing fine teeth in a wide smile. His eyes caught the glint of sun, emphasising their blue brilliance. Her heart quickened, not entirely pleasurably; although it was clear to her he had been waiting for her, which was flattering, there was something — an indefinable quality about him — intimidating — that she found disturbing. Yet his manners were impeccable. He attempted no undue familiarity, expressing only the pleasure it had given him to meet her and the hope that she would pay another visit soon or allow him to call on her at Oaklands.

Her reply was ambiguous.

'Perhaps. But at the moment I think it's better to keep things on a business footing. It's my father, you see—' The lovely eyes raised to his were suddenly alight with warmth and emotion. 'For his sake I need desperately to get the paper's affairs settled.'

'I understand. And if there's anything I can do,' he assured her, 'let me know. Promise?'

She smiled. 'Very well, of course — and thank you.'

As she kicked Lady to a canter she didn't notice the sudden, almost imperceptible tightening of the lips, or the cold ice-blue quality of his stare. Blue — yes, but remote and chilling as the shadows of snow peaks in brilliant sunshine.

He wanted her; to have her under his control as neatly scheduled as the butterflies, pinned in his special collection under glass. A proud young madam, he thought, but he'd have and tame her.

That same evening he surprised his father by announcing calmly, 'The girl you had here — Miss Fairley—'

'Yes?'

'I want to marry her.'

'You — *what*?' Like a bullet from a gun the last word shattered the air.

'I want her for my wife.'

'Then you can damn well want,' Jonathan said roughly. 'When you take a wife it'll be someone of class, and with a good dowry. I'm having no cheeky little nobody in the Bradley family. It wasn't for that you went to Public School and Oxford, so just get that idea out of your head once and for all, lad. It won't be long before the right girl appears, to eat out of your hand when she knows how lucky she is.'

'This one will,' Arthur stated calmly, 'and she's the one I want.'

Eventually Bradley was forced to the conclusion that his heir — a stubborn and odd character, if ever there was one — really meant it.

Well if that was the case, he could do worse, he supposed. He didn't need a woman with cash, and marrying Emma might solve a number of problems.

So the matter was left in abeyance, and as it happened something occurred the following week which tragically solved everything.

2

'I'm drawing out,' Frank Page said bleakly, averting his eyes from William's face as he delivered the blunt statement. 'It's no good, Fairley. Unless we go in with Bradley we've had it. Profit from the *Echo*'s practically nil; in a few months we'll be in debt. Without compromising, that is.'

He raised his eyes slowly to William's face which in those few seconds had paled to ashen grey.

'You mean you want to sell? Every one of them? Every share?'

'I'm afraid so. I'm damned sorry. It's a blow to me, as much to you. Well — you've more to lose — I know that. But facts have to be faced. Without the capital we haven't a chance in a million of winning against Bradley. I'm willing to go along with him — up to a certain point, if you are. But then you're not, obviously.' He paused before adding, 'I take it there's nothing in your kitty to draw on? No personal assets to risk?'

'My property,' William answered honestly. 'That's about all. Oaklands.'

Page looked away again. 'In that case — why don't you call it a day? The *Courier* wants good men — you could get in there any time; I was chatting to Martin Drake the other day, and he as good as told me you'd not be wanting a decent post if you decided to fold up. A good salary, no worries, and the challenge of joining forces against Bradley and his *Comet*. You're respected in the newspaper world, and whatever that jumped-up northern Johnny thinks, his newfangled notions aren't going to affect the *Courier*.'

'Are you sure?'

'To no great extent anyway. He may have power, but it's the new kind. The Wilton family's got generations of traditions and trust — *and* solid currency behind it. If they have to, they'll fight, and win. Mark my words, in another ten years the *Comet* will be wiped out, and Bradley's new-fangled idea of *The Midlander* will be a second-rate memory, no more. You have a future there, old man, if you want it. And maybe a place on the Board. Mind you, I don't *know* but it's well worth following up. I do happen to have eyes and ears in my head, and Tom Wilton's always been a friend of mine.'

'Yes.'

There was a long embarrassed pause until Fairley said dully, 'You mean it, about selling?'

'Sorry. Yes. Unless you care to give Bradley what he wants.'

With sudden force, William, whose temper was generally controlled, jumped up from his chair, knocking the glass of whisky over, so it spilled in a stream across the office table, staining papers of copy waiting to be edited.

'Then go to hell with it,' he said. 'I thought you were a friend, Page; I never thought that in a bad patch you would just let me down. But that's just what you're doing, isn't it? *Isn't* it?'

All colour had left his face again. The knuckles of his clenched fist were very white on the crumpled papers.

'Here, steady on, old man,' Page remonstrated. 'You're not well. Sit down.'

'No thanks. I'm all right.' William reached for his coat from a peg, stiffened and remarked coldly, 'The meeting's over, I think. I'll lock up now, and call it a day. Ready?'

'If you're sure—'

'I'm sure. I know where I stand now. Alone — except for Emma.'

'I was thinking about her as well,' Page said as they went to the door. 'And the other one — Rosalind.'

'They'll be all right. My family's my own concern,' William stated decisively. 'They'll not starve.'

But what *would* they do?

As he drove erratically five minutes later from Charbrook towards the forest road leading to Oaklands, his mind, though whirling, felt empty and dead of ideas or the capacity to make plans.

On impulse, before reaching his home, he made a detour of three miles or so, taking a winding route past Feyland Woods towards Bradgate. Before he faced Emma he felt an urgent necessity to bring his emotions under control so they could discuss the issue together — assess a problem that at the moment appeared not only *un*discussable, but unsolvable.

He must have peace for a brief time, allow the rugged slopes and ancient history of the park to encompass him with the tranquillity and atmosphere of things by-gone. From his earliest youth Bradgate had been his sanctuary during periods of doubt and trouble — soothing over-sensitive nerves to rest and aware-ness of the illusion of Time.

On countless mornings he'd wandered there to hear birdsong as the first streaks of dawn lit the sky. At the knobbly roots of the ancient stunted oaks, where the ill-fated Lady Jane Grey had wandered before the proclamation of being proclaimed queen centuries ago, countless rabbits now had their burrows. At the time of her death, it was said, the trees also had been lopped. But sad events had not robbed the park of its beauty. The stream still trickled gently down the valley past the tumbled ruin; bracken grew thick at the base of the hills — fresh green in the spring, changing with autumn to russet, gold and brown. Deer moved gracefully and unmolested by thickets and up the slopes. Even in rutting time the great antlered stags showed no animosity. It was as though, in solitary hours, Nature's gentle hand had erased all conflict of past history, leaving only a dreaming quiet that had generally eased William's problems and reinforced his inherent energy.

That day, though, seemed a little different. He was more tired than usual; after parking the car and climbing the tricky ladder-like entrance to the domain, he walked only a few hundred yards or so, before the old nagging pain across the chest returned, forcing him to rest. He found a granite boulder, seated himself on it, and gradually the discomfiture passed. How quiet it was — not a breath of wind — only the damp sweet odours of earth and air, and occasional rustle of undergrowth where a rabbit's white tail showed momentarily then disappeared. On his left the shape of 'Old John' depicted by a miniature folly, a castle-like ruin, rose golden-brown, showing darker patches of bog, against the fading sky. He lit his pipe, smiling slightly, as he noted a landmark of a twisted dead tree halfway up the slope; it had been there ever since he was a boy. Emma called it the 'Witch', and as a child had woven fairy tales about it. 'P'raps she put a spell on poor Lady Jane,' his young daughter had suggested once when she was a little girl, 'and that's why she had her head cut off. Oh Papa — d'you think she's a ghost now, like the people say? D'you think she's happy?'

William had squeezed the small hand comfortingly.

'Wherever she is, she's all right,' he'd said. 'And you mustn't think of ghosts and witches. Look at that baby fawn over there—'

Diverted, Emma's attention had been drawn to the graceful animal shapes moving by a cluster of silver birch. But a curious sadness had stirred William's thoughts, and it was the same this evening, as he stared reflectively over the landscape. It wasn't difficult, in the fitful light, to imagine the frail ethereal shape of a young girl drifting soundlessly from her ruined home down the curving drive; perhaps, indeed, something of her spirit did remain there, imbuing the area with mystery and regret.

He pulled himself together with a jerk.

What was the matter with him? Soliloquising with himself like any sentimental woman. He must be leaving and return to Oaklands. Even at his home there was business for him to tackle, and Rosalind would be wanting to say goodnight before she went to bed.

As usual, his heart lurched when he thought of her. So beautiful to look at — fair like her mother, but incapable of a normal existence. He'd tried to love her, but it was difficult; his emotions were too complicated, and the thought of her future a constant worry. He sighed, tapped the bowl of his pipe on the granite, and forced the uncharacteristic vague mood from him.

The *Echo*!

Oaklands? — What to do?

His name was good at the bank, of course; he could get a mortgage on his old home. There *were* ways of keeping the *Echo* and its *Weekly* going. But ultimate survival was a different matter. And William had a fierce objection to shouldering loans which eventually might force him to bankruptcy. He had a little over two weeks left to solve the challenge, and with Bradley as opponent, he couldn't see a hope of winning.

Oh well! be damned to them! he'd soldier on to the last, and after that? Who could tell? How could any human being in the world really count on what the next week or even day would bring? Life was chancy anyway. Emma would have her mother's small capital when he went, and he had sufficient faith in his daughter's stubborn courage to know she'd somehow manage to look after Rosalind. So there was no point in worrying; none at all.

He got up, feeling suddenly better and released from strain. As he turned to take the steep path past a fenced spinney to the summit of the hill, he drew a deep breath. A rush of vigour stirred his blood. He lifted his chin to the sky, noted a last streak of dying daylight catch the tip of the folly; then — unpredictably, the earth seemed to sway beneath his feet. All round him trees, rocks, and the startled movements of a deer wheeled into a vortex of whirling darkness. There was a return of the cutting pain across his chest. He clutched his tweed jacket along the heart, gulped vainly for more air. It was no use.

As he tottered and fell a bird rose, squawking from the bracken nearby, and took flight towards the stretch of moor where the twisted form of the blackened old tree stood stark against its boggy pool.

Hours later a gamekeeper found him. He was lying on his back with his lifeless eyes staring at the sky.

When Emma heard, her first wild grief gradually turned to a cold deadly determination for vindication and resolve to avenge her father's death.

By whatever means, she swore to herself, the *Echo* and Oaklands would both survive. Somehow she'd beat the hateful

Bradleys and see that Fairley traditions were upheld, and endured. Never, *never* would the northern upstart get his fists on Fairley territory.

Just how her end would be achieved she couldn't visualise. Neither, at that point, did she try. Her emotions were too poignantly involved, finding, after the first tormented reactions, relief only in solitude and tears.

3

Both Jonathan Bradley and his son, Arthur, made a point of attending William's funeral which took place at the nearest church standing only half a mile from Oaklands in the centre of a small hamlet, Woodley.

Arthur's brilliant cold eyes strayed briefly once or twice to Emma's rigid form. She was wearing grey, knowing that William would have fiercely resented his daughter appearing as some dreary crow dressed all in black. She appeared tearless and completely composed during the sad ceremony; no trace of emotion belied her inner distress. She could have been an ice-maiden, Arthur thought, noting the set, exquisite profile. Even the rich fire of her hair was hidden under her hat. Her remoteness did not disturb him in the least. He didn't care for emotional over-wrought women; their vapours, moods, vagaries, everlasting demands and cravings for attention filled him with distaste. At one period, when he was young, he recalled how his mother had fretted and yearned for romance and affection from his father, and the ironic way in which he'd thwarted her. She'd been pretty then, in a rather plump, over-luscious way, which had been, Arthur discovered, the only reason for the union — well, at the base of it.

Jonathan had been foolish enough to fall for her charms when

she worked at his father's mill — an affair ending in an un-
wanted pregnancy leading to a completely unsuitable marriage.
Still, Amelia had done her best to fill the dutiful role of wife to
the ambitious Jonathan. What she wanted he'd seen that she
had, in reason, and in return she'd learned to keep out of the
way when he wished, occupying his bed only when he crudely
demanded it, which had become almost nil these days. For
appearances' sake she appeared with him when necessary at
social functions, and had learned to keep her Yorkshire brogue
at a low ebb. She had been a good mother, and ran the house
efficiently. Any brief 'affairs' he indulged in in no way interfered with her status, and were very rare. She might be hurt on
such occasions, but she didn't show it. Her husband had her
firmly trained in what was expected of her. She feared his
temper, though it was always cold, and he'd never harmed or
touched her. As a woman she had become a mere useful necessity in the running of Eastwood, and her son further despised her
as much as his father did.

He knew he would never despise Emma; that was one reason
why he was determined to possess her, to have her, like some
exotic yet cool jewel in his possession, for gazing at, touching,
and exhibiting when it suited him.

A week following William's funeral, he rode over to Oaklands
to pay, presumably, a social visit, and one expressing his concern and sympathy.

Emma happened to be in the garden when he arrived, cutting
a few last autumn leaves for the house. She was wearing green,
of a dark olive shade that suited the rusty gleam of her molten
hair. Her form was outlined elegantly against the winter foliage,
her face pale and rather ethereal in the transient light.

Arthur doffed his bowler and swung himself from his saddle.
With his hand at the gelding's bridle, he gave a little bow, came
towards her, and said, 'Miss Fairley — Emma — I do hope I'm
not precipitate in making a call to ask how you are? And of
course once again offer my sympathy.' He came towards her, his
hand extended. Reluctantly she let him take hers.

'I'm as well as can be expected, Mr Bradley,' she told him

with no trace of a smile. 'My father's death is a great loss. But—' her voice quivered slightly, '—his work has to go on.'

'You mean the *Echo*?'

She sighed. A spray of copper beech dropped from her grasp and fell to the damp earth. He bent down quickly, retrieved it and handed it to her.

'Of course.' Her voice was low, determined, and bitter. 'It's the only thing I can do for him now. Carry on.'

She glanced away. He touched her shoulder lightly. 'Emma—'

'*Please!* Don't.' With a sharp motion she jerked herself free.

'Very well. But there's something I'd like to talk over with you – if you can spare the time.'

She whirled round, facing him with rising colour, and a widening of her clear grey eyes. The brilliant blue flame of his own never faltered. 'I don't see what there *can* be between you and me to discuss,' she said coldly. 'The position of the *Echo* with you and Mr Bradley has already been made brutally clear. It's what killed my father.'

'A very cruel thing to say. But you naturally feel resentment. However, you're wrong, quite wrong about *one* thing. It wasn't my wish not to support William Fairley on his own terms. On the contrary I'd have been co-operative. It's been quite an achievement of his keeping the paper's character alive for so many years. I respect his will and determination, although if I'd been a member of the board I might have suggested a few alterations.'

Her astonishment was so great she didn't speak for some seconds, then she asked quietly, 'What, Mr Bradley?'

'Arthur,' he corrected her.

'Arthur then.'

'May we go into the house?' he suggested. 'Or would you rather walk a short way down the lane? That would be better perhaps, as I have Kismet, and it will cause less gossip than in the house.' He smiled faintly and patted his mount's neck.

She hesitated, but only for a moment. 'Very well. Although I really don't see the point. Any suggestion you had concerning the *Echo* is useless now. And I can't understand—'

'Of course you can't,' he interrupted. 'But my idea would have involved you very much, Emma. My father doesn't agree with me I know, but I believe the feminine viewpoint of your own column, and the space could be considerably extended. You have the will, the style, and knowledge of the locality that could make a talking point of the publication given a fair chance.'

She was astounded.

'If you could have got *your* father to see it when mine was alive, things might have worked out,' she reminded him. 'It seems so futile even talking about it now, when — when — oh I really do think we're wasting time, don't you?'

'No.' The short word silenced her. 'Come, please — just a few yards. I beg of you—'

'*You* beg me — how *very* ridiculous!'

All the same, with the hem of her skirt lifted in one hand, she found herself a moment or two later following him through the gate down the lane.

By a gate in a recess leading to a farm, he stopped, took her arm gently, and together, with the gelding on one side they moved towards the field.

She didn't glance at him. Her face was turned resolutely on the rutted track and dip in pasture land on either side before it dipped towards the woods, but his blue eyes were keen and covertly on her intriguing profile, the gentle swelling of breasts above the tiny waist, and proud, inaccessible lift of chin.

'Emma,' he said, after a short pause.

'Yes?'

'I want to marry you.'

'*Marry?*' Her mind for a moment was stupefied.

'I said so.'

She frowned, staring at him in astonishment. 'But you don't know me. We've hardly met. We've nothing in common. Nothing at all.'

'Haven't we?'

'Well—' Quick as lightning, after the first hesitation her thoughts leaped ahead, forming some kind of wild out-of-the-world plan that suddenly made cold clear sense. If he meant it — if his reckless proposal was genuine — couldn't it provide the answer to her problem? She didn't love him, no; but he was madly attractive and handsome, and if she was clever could be brought round probably with giving the support financially, for the *Echo*'s survival. In time possibly, her emotions would respond naturally to his. Many women made success of unions founded on convenience, and this one wouldn't be *entirely* that. From their first meeting she'd been fascinated, against her will by the enigmatic spectacular son of the greedy tycoon from the North. Arthur himself was cultured and educated, with sensitivity under his elegant facade which she had not suspected. He was entranced by her, he must be, or he would not have made this very reckless declaration.

'Well, Emma?' she heard him saying in slightly husky undertones.

Her cheeks, when she faced him, were faintly tinged with pink, holding the quality of sunlight shining through the texture of some delicate pale shell.

'I'll have to think,' she said quietly, though her heart was beating fiercely.

'Why?'

Staring into the ice-blue pools of his cold brilliant eyes, reason died into sudden abandoned acceptance. What had she to lose after all? Only gain could come from such a marriage, and vindication of her father's death — proof of his faith in her. Little by little she'd learn how to wind Arthur Bradley round her little finger. Then the *Echo* and Oaklands would be safe.

'Very well,' she managed to say in controlled even tones. 'All right, I'll marry you, Arthur.'

He attempted to kiss her, but she pushed him away.

'Later,' she said. 'You must give me the chance to face what I'm doing, and—'

'Yes?'

'There are things we have to discuss, aren't there? About the paper I mean, and—'

He was slightly chagrined, but did his best not to show it. 'Just as you say, business woman,' he remarked, with an odd smile on his mouth belying inward irritation. Let her plot and plan in any way she liked, he thought, about her ineffectual little newspaper rag. What she wanted there, she could have, in reason. And he, in his turn, would take what he wanted of her when the time came.

So the matter was settled.

In January of the following year Emma Fairley and Arthur Bradley were married. The *Echo*, reimbursed, flourished under the Fairley name still, and Oaklands was made permanently financially secure as Emma's private property to be used and lived in whenever she liked, for holiday periods or when Arthur was away on business.

Those were her conditions.

His proved to be very different.

*

Their bridal night was spent at a luxurious Bournemouth hotel prior to the couple's fortnight's visit to the Continent the next day. Their special suite was magnificent, commanding a wide view of the coast, the furnishings lavish, even exotic, subtly contrived to induce an air of romance. Deep rose-pink velvet, crystal and gold, with all the embellishments of a mediaeval fairy tale provided an extravagant background for the new young wife. The hotel service, if obsequious, was flatteringly conscious of the desire for complete privacy and immediate attention at the tinkle of a bell. Royalty could not have wished for more. They retired early. There were two separate dressing-rooms. Emma at last emerged from hers, clad in a cream satin gown patterned with small hand-embroidered roses. No princess could have looked lovelier. Lace swathed her shoulders, and bordered her negligée. Her hair was loose, and in the light from the crystal wall chandeliers glimmered burnished rich auburn. The lines of her breasts and thighs were clearly definable under the soft material — the cream of her skin only a shade warmer than the cream of her attire.

A glance in the cheval mirror had told her she looked lovely, so she had no lack of confidence when she pushed the door open and stepped on to the thick pile of the pink bedroom carpet.

She was a virgin, having no knowledge of sex at all, except what her instincts told her, and her innate innocence somehow gave her additional fey beauty. Her trousseau had cost her more than she could afford as Emma Fairley, but at Aden's — Feyland's most select costumiers — she had bowed to the wisdom of Madam Elana who ran the establishment, and who had cunningly implied the great importance of a young wife's first intimate impact on a husband.

Besides — a *Bradley*! A future Bradley had no need to spare expense.

The knowledge, to Emma, had had a heady, slightly unreal feeling about it. But now she was thankful for her extravagance, and when she saw Arthur in his blue robe come towards her, doubly so. Her heart quickened, not with love, but expectancy. She knew the rules of marriage, through having dealt with and reviewed so much literature on behalf of the *Echo*. One must appear willing, but not too obviously so. The woman *always* must be pursued. Shyness, a slight trepidation was acceptable, and in this case would be genuine. Already, though, her body, from tension, was relaxing. Arthur and she might not be exactly soul-mates, but oh! how very handsome he was.

She waited, with a queer mixture of alternating emotions in her, for him to take her in his arms. His blue eyes were so very bright, so concentrated, and — desirous was it? Or merely admiring?

She said nothing. Beneath the satin the quick thudding of her heart was visible. He took a swift stride towards her, drew her hand to his lips, then bent down and kissed the hem of her gown.

When he got up his face was blazing, not with affection, but with pride of possession.

'You are beautiful,' he said, 'gorgeous, my Emma.'

She stared as he touched her waist and let his fingers slide up her arm gently. 'You are more perfect even than my shepherdess – my exquisite little French piece—' he broke off. His smile was a little twisted, his eyes colder than coldest glass. 'So when you see my collection – my china masterpiece—'

She pulled her hand away abruptly, drawing her lacy wrap closer against her neck.

'What do you mean? Your collection? Aren't you going to – aren't we—?'

'Man and wife, darling? Of course we are. We shall sleep together, dance – ride; anything you wish to do and have you can – in reason. But—' he paused.

'Yes?' Her voice was suddenly shrill, unnatural.

He sighed.

'I do hope you're not going to be old-fashioned, Emma. Old-fashioned people are so deadly *boring*.' He moved away to the dressing table, took a cigarette from a gold case and lit it, theatrically. Then he turned and blew a smoke ring into the air.

'Do you understand, darling?'

'No. I don't think so.'

'Ah. A pity.'

She lifted her head challengingly. 'What is it you're trying to imply, Arthur?'

The smile on his thin lips died. 'Do I have to spell it out? Are you so naive?'

'I think I am, in certain ways,' she told him bluntly. 'And I think you *do* have to spell it out. I suppose—' her voice faltered slightly, '—I suppose the gist of it is that you *don't* really want me at all – physically. You're not interested in *me*, in having children, and a normal married life. You're just—'

'Well? Go on.' His command was steel cold, like his eyes.

She paused before daring to say at last, 'Abnormal in some way.'

He gave a little bow. 'Thank you. You've hit it, exactly. But in one way you're wrong. I do want you, Emma, because I prize beauty, with the same zest as I detest the conventional dull-as-ditchwater business of a man and woman doomed to the rules and regulations — of cohabitation. A messy business, I always think. All right for morons and the animals, but for an exquisite creature such as you — somehow offensive. Don't mistake me—' He touched her cheek lightly for a second, then pressed his lips against her shoulder fleetingly, 'You are lovely — you smell sweet and are quite bewitching, I love, adore you very much, in my own fashion. I'm sure we shall get along very well. You will be the elegant Mrs Arthur Bradley and the envy of society—'

'I shall also be owner of Oaklands, and of the *Echo*,' she cut in tartly and very clearly, pulling herself away firmly, dazed and humiliated still, but clinging to the one card she still held.

'Partly, I think.'

'More than partly,' she flashed, 'I shall hold you to it, and you'll see there's no interference from your father or I'll make you the laughing stock and scorn of Leyfordshire—'

'In which case—' he smiled cruelly, 'I might have to take a switch to your back, madam. I'm no weakling, you know.'

She shivered. He put an arm round her and said more gently, 'Emma, I didn't want a scene, and there's no reason, really, for such melodrama. I may be an odd — unique — kind of fellow, but you're not — sexually in love with me, are you? In marrying me there was quite a good deal of self-interest on your part. Then why can't you allow me the pleasure of admiring you and making you the pride of the county? — And mine?'

She shook her head slowly, and went to the bed flinging herself face down on the satin spread. He went over to the window, parted the curtain and stared out to sea. A moon was rising, lighting the quivering surface of the water to rippling gold.

'It's going to be fine in the morning,' she heard him saying matter-of-factly. 'Come to bed, Emma. You must feel rested for the Channel crossing.'

Presently she moved reluctantly and obeyed. They lay side by side; the bed was warm, the firelight played intriguingly round walls and ceiling. But without realising it her teeth chattered. She was cold. From time to time during the night she felt him touch her, and she moved involuntarily closer. There was no response. He gave a grunt, and turned away. For all he cared, she realised bitterly, she could have been a piece of marble, or stone.

And for that, she hated him.

In the morning early tea and breakfast were brought up to them. There was a knowing glint in the waitress's eye when she'd drawn the curtains and deposited the trays on the side tables.

'I hope you were comfortable, madam? Sir?' she said, envisaging amorous events of a rich honeymoon.

'Very comfortable, thank you,' Emma heard herself replying coolly.

'Good. If there is anything more you require—'

'There's nothing,' Arthur answered shortly.

The maid withdrew discreetly.

Arthur smiled down at his wife.

'You look very young,' he said, 'with your hair loose like that. Today perhaps you should wear a chignon under the sailor hat, the one in your box. There may be a breeze over the Channel.'

A sailor hat? It seemed somehow ludicrous. Recalling the fresh cold winds rustling through the woods of Burnwood on her face and through her tumbled locks, Emma felt a wild, almost overwhelming, longing to be back at her old home in the forest – free to wade barefoot through the cool streams, or wander up Hawkshill to the iron age settlement where she'd played and pretended as a child. But those days were gone now. She was Mrs Arthur Bradley. What irony. Thank heaven she hadn't really been in love with him. Supposing though – before the question really formulated in her mind, she smothered it resolutely. No one could have everything. A husband's natural love might be denied her, but Oaklands and the paper remained. She had saved them, for her father's sake. Did he guess? Was there such a thing, really, as immortality?

Oh yes, she told herself resolutely, there must be, somehow, in some way, however frail the spark might be. In no other way, now, could her life be justified.

The day went as planned, and the fortnight following they visited Holland, Italy, France, and Switzerland. Arthur proved himself a courteous companion, attentive in public, in private mostly remote and reflective. Once she was tempted to say bitterly, 'You must show me your shepherdess when we return to Eastwood, Arthur. Your prize-piece. I hope I'll be able to bear the comparison.'

After a brief glance at her tight expression he answered coldly, 'There's no need to be nasty, Emma, or jealous. You must learn to prize beauty for its own sake. As I do.'

She had a quick impulse to slap his face, but restrained herself.

'I already do, or I should not have married you, should I?'

'For your *Echo* you would,' he told her. 'Your conscience is a very flexible one, darling.'

She didn't reply. Such arguments after all were not only ineffectual, but cheap.

So time passed, a period during which most of the sights and grand landscapes of Europe were absorbed.

On their eventual return to Leyfordshire, the newly married couple found a reception prepared for them having all the trappings and extravaganza considered suitable for the emotional culmination of young love's union.

There was a warily expectant gleam in Jonathan's eyes, expressing the hope a son might have been conceived. Obviously, Emma thought, he had very little practical knowledge of his own son's potentials, or lack of them.

And she considered how she was going to bear it.

4

Following the return of his son and young wife to Eastwood from
the Continent, Jonathan found himself appreciating Emma
more than he would have believed possible before their marriage. In her he soon recognised qualities that mildly astonished
him. She was a stronger character than he'd imagined, more
remote and dignified than was usual in one so young. He'd been
aware, of course, of her natural impetuosity, at their first
meeting, when she'd challenged him and fought for the *Echo* on
her father's behalf. But this Emma Fairley — or rather Emma
Bradley — was quite different. She had slipped into the role of
mistress of the establishment as easily as slipping her slim hand
into a glove. Of course, Amelia, as his wife, still reigned,
nominally. She had indeed over-dressed herself absurdly to
emphasise the fact. But to his discerning eye, she too was
impressed, refraining for a time, even, from her secret tippling,
in order to keep a clear head with the capacity to put the young
madam in her place.

Jonathan was amused. The domestic situation brought diver-
sion to the more dull moments when he was confined to the
house. Jessie, on the other hand, his daughter, saw nothing to
smile about. She was a rather plain girl who had unfortunately
inherited the weaker points in appearance of both parents,
having Jonathan's square, rather hard, jaw and solid build, and
her mother's indifferent features without her pretty colouring.

She was just seventeen, and was going as a boarder to a select
finishing school in France the following year.

Emma tried to be nice to her, but it was difficult. Jessie simply
had no charm, and from the beginning had been jealous of her
brother's wife. The fact tickled Arthur's cruel sense of humour.

'Don't give up, old girl,' he said playfully once. 'Dress yourself up more, get a new riding habit and swing a leg before Roly Plummer. Got his eye on you already. Some men are like that — have a penchant for a nice plump rump—' he laughed mockingly.

'You beast. You vulgar creature,' Jessie cried. 'If Papa heard you talk like that — or that simpering wife of yours—'

'Ah, but he won't, neither will she,' he said meaningfully. 'You know quite well, sister dear, I'm an adept at suiting my conversation to my company.'

Jessie snorted and turned away.

'I don't know how she sticks you.'

'She's a highly intelligent woman,' he replied adroitly, thinking at the same time, too intelligent by half sometimes for his own comfort. The way, after only a week, she'd wormed her way into his father's interest, baffled him. She'd already, with his — Arthur's help — got what she wanted — a percentage of decisive shareholdings in the *Echo*, and a whole page on the weekly edition for her women's feature. That old house of rock was hers for all time, and Rosalind, her half-baked young sister, was safely settled there with the housekeeper and a young woman acting as a governess-cum-nurse, who to his mind was a damned unnecessary expense. She should have been put in a home. But he had never suggested it, knowing Emma might have left him on the spot.

Emma! Frequently he smiled wrily when thinking of her. At the moment she seemed to have the upper hand of him. But she'd better not flaunt the fact too openly. He had a smart little buggy-whip in his cupboard which he'd certainly use if she went too far. She was his possession. He'd *bought* her. She knew it, he knew it, and so did his father. But as days passed and Emma's presence grew more potent at Eastwood he came to the conclusion they should move to a separate establishment. There was a Dower House on the estate which could be made exotically comfortable, where their private life would not be too pried on by his astute father.

Emma received the suggestion agreeably. 'Yes,' she said, 'I

quite agree. We *should* have our own house. Another thing, Arthur—'

'Yes?'

Her grey eyes were straight and clear on his face when she said, 'I think I should spend one day and two nights a week at Oaklands.'

He stared at her, his blue eyes narrowed and cold. 'For heaven's sake why? If you expect me to traipse every week to that godforsaken hole—'

'I don't expect you to, Arthur.' Her voice was cold and clipped. 'I happen to have a sister who needs a little of my company. Whereas you – you don't *really* need me at all, do you? – Except to stare at me and touch for your odious little abnormal games, and to show me off to your friends?'

Her voice had a sneer in it.

He flushed.

'You're my wife, madam.'

'*Am* I?' The implication of the question did not escape him.

'*Yes*. And you will do as I say.'

'I've had no chance not to, have I? Not yet,' she remarked icily. 'Whatever you've wanted of me – mostly – you've taken, however unpleasant or warped it might be—'

'Warped? Did you say *warped*?' His face had gone very red.

'Most people would think so.'

'Most people? If—'

She waved a hand contemptuously. 'Oh, don't worry, Arthur. I don't intend to reveal your secret. On the other hand, I expect you to respect my wish concerning Oaklands.'

Eventually, Arthur grudgingly agreed.

Jonathan was mildly perturbed.

'*Every* weekend seems rather demanding,' he said to his son, not adding, 'the thin end of the wedge,' which he thought.

'It needn't work out that way,' Arthur remarked casually, 'in any case I've planned something else for the future.'

'Oh? *What?*'

Arthur explained his idea for the Dower House, and although Jonathan didn't at first agree, he was brought round to accepting it, when his son pointed out how very eccentric Amelia was becoming since his marriage. 'You can't have two women queening it in a house,' he said. 'Mama's not only showing off and making herself look a fool to the servants and everyone else, she's getting irritable and snappy. And that evening when the Darnleys came, she looked *ludicrous*! Absolutely. Her make-up! Well, for heaven's sake! You must've noticed. Her accent too — she never stopped talking, and it was all just to be one up on Emma. You've got to stop that, Pater, or your chances of getting into Parliament for the next term are nil.'

Jonathan was shocked by the observation, but when he'd had time to think things over, he saw that his son was right. It was essential he became accepted by the 'gentry' — the aristocratic horsey crowd and their associates who had mansions and hunting boxes dotted about that particular area of Leyfordshire. In time, with tact, an acceptable display of wealth, and generous donations to various charities and good causes he felt certain he could do it, provided Amelia was kept on a low key. As a potential future MP he needed support from the local party. The constituency had always been conservative. Alfred Carstairs, who was now an old man and not fit had already declared openly that at the next election he would not put up again, therefore it was up to Jonathan to create an acceptable public image before the crucial date arrived. The new radical lot would have no chance at all. A liberal just *might* — providing he had a sufficiently impressive background and sponsorship. That mustn't happen. Neither, Jonathan decided, must any other conservative be allowed to put himself against him, provided he could be dissuaded. Studying the position from every angle, Bradley came to the conclusion that the odds of his own support were encouragingly favourable, especially with the backing of his press — the Leyford *Comet*, and with luck and a little co-operation from Emma, the Charbrook *Echo*. The latter, he knew, might be tricky, but provided he was clever enough to win his daughter-in-law's approval, quite possible. She was now one of the Bradley family, and would recognise with her characteristic honesty that this fact alone demanded a certain duty from her; loyalty. He'd have to be careful not to tread on her toes, as they put it, where her late father was concerned. She would have extra space if she wanted it for her high-falutin' feminine and women's talk. He wouldn't cross her at any forthcoming Board Meetings. It would be a battle of wits — subtle, very subtle. But in the end he'd have what mattered of the *Echo*'s circulation in his pocket. Yes, he must cultivate Emma; with the combined papers working on his behalf, his influence would stretch across the county. He had also managed to be on friendly terms with Lord Wendle, which should be helpful.

He'd show them.

The old fashioned *Courier* wouldn't have a chance. Strictly non-political, over-rational when anything sensational rocked society, its influence would sink to a minimum. In time the *Midlander* would emerge, as he'd envisaged during the past two years. He, Jonathan Bradley, would be the one Newspaper Magnate of the area.

And after that? Wild dreams surged through his mind of a knighthood and eventually possible elevation to the peerage.

If only Amelia was equal to raising herself. If only he'd had more sense and less honour than to marry her following the disastrous affair of his youth. If it hadn't been for the warm night, honeysuckle scent, and the luscious white body half bursting from her bodice, she'd have been back at the Mill the next day, without a further thought from him. It was only by chance the thing had happened anyway. There'd been a dance and get-together at the village hall, celebrating his grandfather's birthday. Most of the employees had been there and in a weak moment afterwards, Jonathan had walked her home.

Home! A humble, but spotless cottage under the moor, where Amelia had been rigorously brought up by strict hard-working parents. At the time he'd been lusty and hot with life, and before taking her safely inside, the sweetness and scent of her had been too much for him. He'd had her in the bracken, with her hair spilled pale gold in the moonlight, her white thighs ripe and ready for his ravishing. He seldom remembered the occasion now, and when he did he was mildly ashamed — until he also thought of Arthur, who'd been the fruit of their union. A fine specimen he was now — to look at. But what was he *really* like, inside? Jonathan had never quite been able to fathom his son's mind or ways. He'd gone to public school and Oxford, yet still remained an enigma — sarcastic often, a little contemptuous of himself and others, though why, heaven alone knew. He had everything he wanted, with a clever, spectacular wife now, into the bargain.

Was the marriage all right?

At times Jonathan wondered. There seemed something — ambiguous, for want of a better word — between them, that he couldn't fathom. It could be purely imagination, of course; he hoped so, because Emma's co-operation could mean a good deal to him in the future.

Therefore he made no objection when, a month after the wedding, Emma left Eastwood for a weekend at Oaklands.

She drove herself in the Mercedes, which she'd insisted on retaining at her new home. Arthur had been mildly amused, Jonathan irritated, to see her sitting at the wheel of such a ramshackle uncertain thing. In fact, he didn't approve of any woman in control of transport unless it was a lady-like little governess cart pulled by a well-trained amiable mare on social visits or for charitable means in the district. However, he held his tongue, thinking, why the hell couldn't the girl have used his own chauffeur and the Rolls?

Certainly the journey would have been more comfortable and easier. Twice the engine of William's car stopped, and three miles down a lane from Feyland, Emma had to get the help of a farm labourer to crank it up and get it moving again.

It was midday when she reached Oaklands. Rosalind, wearing a pale blue woollen coat — Emma's first present to her following her marriage — was taken into the garden by the governess as the familiar grinding of the car sounded from the turn down the slope. That day in late February was chilly, but in sheltered spots close to the hedgerows aconites and the pale gold buds of celandines were already starring the lush pulsing brown earth. Certain trees of the forest were feathered by pale green, and as she walked down the path Emma's perceptive ears caught the faint tremor of bird song. Her heart lifted. How lovely to be back.

'Hullo, Rosalind,' she said, holding out her arms. The child didn't run to her in welcome. There was no response at all. She simply stood, looking incredibly lovely like some small princess from a fairy tale, fair hair loose about her shoulders, enormous violet eyes raised to Emma in curious, acquiescent bewilderment.

Emma knelt down and drew her close. The child allowed herself to be kissed, then pulled back, hiding her face against Helen Carly — the governess's — grey woollen dress.

Emma's heart smote her. Had she been recognised? Perhaps — vaguely; but it was impossible to know. Her young sister as always clung only to things of habit, and brief contacts that were forgotten the next moment, as she was diverted by the sight of a bird fluttering from a branch, or a leaf borne on the wind. There was no continuity of her mind. She would never grow up, and would always be a responsibility to others. No wonder William had despaired frequently and found it hard not to resent the presence of one so helpless who'd cost his beloved wife her life.

Emma released her sister, thinking philosophically, 'She hasn't missed me. I'm not really important to her any more.'

The thought faintly hurt at first, until she reminded herself that the fact would enable her to slip over on Sunday and see Will Clarke, acting business manager of the *Echo*. The News Editor had resigned recently, following Page's withdrawal, and Clarke at the moment had journalistic responsibilities on his own shoulders. There would have to be a new editor of the publication. A board meeting had already been arranged for the following week. Bradley would attend of course; he'd informed Emma he had a very likely man for the job in view. 'Go ahead, but pliable to reasonable suggestions,' he'd told Emma. 'I think we should consider his application carefully.'

'Of course,' Emma had agreed, although she was already

prepared to stand out against her father-in-law if there was the slightest sign of collusion or pre-united policy. She herself had insisted on being informed of any likely candidates hoping for the post. One interested her — a Welshman, Evan Lloyd, with wide experience as a reporter on a daily paper in Monmouthshire. He was not only a journalist, but a writer who'd had one book, a fiery commentary on current society, published, as well as a number of vigorously individual poems in minor but cultural magazines and periodicals. A man obviously of ideas and imagination, she'd thought, who might serve the *Echo* well. A naturalist too. She liked that. His Celtic ancestry — apart from a Welsh father, his mother had been Cornish — titillated the inherent romantic streak beneath her practical facade. Although they'd never met, his image was familiar to her from occasional press photographs. A fine head, with a wide brow, fly-away rebellious brown hair, a whimsical firm mouth above a cleft chin, and that hint of defiance in stance and expression suggesting he might very well eventually become a force in some sphere or the other.

Lively. Alert. A man after her father's own heart. Or *was* he? Was it more a matter of feminine instinct? She would never have admitted the latter possibility — even to herself. After all, when the crucial point arose personalities must be secondary to capacity and suitability for the post. She must be fair, and would be. So with her mind firmly set in this direction, she set off for Will Clarke's home, which was only four miles out of Feyland, near Marten Pool. If he chanced to be at Charbrook working overtime at the offices, she'd make a day of it, have a snack at the Windmill Inn on the way, and then take the main road to the town.

She did not have to. As she circled to the far side of the lake and reached the drive leading to the house, she spotted Clarke, fishing, only a hundred yards or so away. She stopped the car, jumped out, and hurried towards him. He was a short, quiet-looking middle-aged man, wearing tweeds and deerstalker.

'My dear Emma,' he said, getting up and coming to greet her. 'How nice to see you.'

She grinned mischievously, shaking her mane of russet hair back, looking suddenly very young indeed.

'Hullo, Mr Clarke. I hope I've not disturbed your fishing.'

He smiled, shaking his head. 'None to disturb. Not biting today. It's no matter though. A pleasure to see you, my dear. Had a meal yet? If not, you must come in and join us. Lucy would be pleased.'

'No thank you, ' she replied, 'really. I'm not hungry. This visit's a sort of spur-of-the-moment idea. The day was fine, and I wanted to see Rosalind. You too. And Oaklands of course.'

'*Ah*. Yes. You must miss it — or don't you? Being a young married lady now.'

'Oh yes I miss it,' she answered, more solemnly than he'd expected. '*Terribly*.'

'Hm!' He looked non-committal. 'Everything going well in your aristocratic establishment, I hope?'

She forced a bright smile. 'Naturally. I wish I was nearer Charbrook though. There's so much to discuss, and with the editor leaving, on top of Mr Page, you must be finding a lot to do.'

'True enough. But we get through. Burley's a great help, and Craddock, the sports editor's a good all-rounder, always willing to lend a hand. I took today off though, as you see. Nothing like a rod and line to ease the mind.' He paused before adding, 'You want to see me about something, don't you, Emma? What is it? The application?'

'Yes,' she said, and after learning from him that he'd as yet formulated no definite opinion concerning the possibility of names submitted for the *Echo*'s new editorship, managed subtly nevertheless to draw that of Evan Lloyd into the conversation.

Clarke was silent for a moment, then he remarked, 'A fiery customer — sharp-witted and clever, with a way about him. Call it charm, if you like. Oh yes, he's got that. Have you met him?'

'No.'

'Hm. I *have*, and was impressed. But for the *Echo*? I'm not sure, Emma; and I'm not at all certain he's the man your father would have backed. The *Echo*'s got to pull its socks up — we all know that. But to *jerk* them! — personally I'm not at all sure William would have approved.'

'No. Neither am I.'

Clarke's eyebrows shot up. 'Well then — why Lloyd?'

Emma's grey eyes lighted on Will's face directly. Something in their very clear straight gaze mildly disconcerted him.

'On most things my father and I thought alike,' she said after a short pause, 'but he was perhaps a little too conservative — even too honourable.' Again the mischievous look on the intriguing impish mouth. 'I think we have to explore new channels, Mr Clarke, and liven things up a bit.'

Will shrugged. 'You have the casting vote, to put it bluntly. And no doubt if you're determined for us to take on Lloyd, you'll succeed, in the end. You may be right at that. I wouldn't fight you.'

'Well, we shall see. After all, I'm only *one* voice. And truly I *will* be fair.'

He knew she'd try to be, but he also sensed that she'd get her way.

Which she did.

5

Jonathan's first reaction when Emma insisted on Evan Lloyd's name being put forward on the short list for the *Echo*, was to object. His instinct was to be wary of Celtic races, especially the Welsh, and the fellow already had a name for being a rebel and far too eager to seize the news of any project he was interested in. True, originality, and a go-ahead character were desirable for the paper's future, and incidentally his, Jonathan's. But not *too* original. He was surprised at Emma's stubborn support for

Lloyd. Arthur, he considered, had made a mistake in persuading him to allow her so much power. And he himself had been weak in giving in. But he'd never imagined any woman could be so pigheaded, or that she would risk bringing discord into the Bradley family now she was a member of it. It was her duty to support his wishes. In allowing her a ruling power of shareholdings he'd trusted her. They both had — he and his son. In a way he'd given in to bribery, because Arthur desired the little chit so much. Now see where it had got them both — a young woman setting her will against the judgement of the Board. Well — perhaps not *all*. Clarke seemed agreeable to taking on the Welshman, and maybe he'd have the support of the other two, Blake and Siddons, when it came to the vote.

There were too many with minor holdings for such a comparatively small newspaper, he thought irritably. Even so, Emma, by *one share* only, could defeat them all if she wanted.

The thought angered and shamed him. He'd been bought out. But then what man in his senses would have expected a twenty-year-old girl to take such an infernal interest in the running of an obscure county newspaper like the *Echo*? He'd expected her to be dutifully concerned with her new life at Eastwood, as Arthur's wife. Yet here she was, still fanatically dedicated to a dead man's ambitions — if they *could* have been William's, and this he doubted. William had been the conservative retiring type, not looking for trouble. But this girl was ready for trouble if it came her way. You could see it in the flash of her eyes and set of her chin when she argued. Well — in view of this he'd have to use subtler means, and apparently go along with her until a way was found to mould policy to his own ends.

It could be done.

If the Welshman came and appeared dangerous in any way — politically or socially, he'd find the means of getting him out!

Damn it all! It was *his* backing and money — Bradley brass — that was keeping the *Echo* going at all. Why didn't Arthur make the point clear to his wife? Remind her just where she stood? What sort of a husband was he? Sometimes Jonathan sensed uncomfortably that things weren't exactly as they should be between them. If so, whose fault was it? Emma's or Arthur's? He tried against his better judgement to blame the woman. She should have been *grateful* for family generosity. But there was something about his son — a streak of oddness he'd never understood, or even particularly tried to. His own passion had always been straightforward — simple, if sometimes crude. But Arthur was devious — the result, he supposed, of public school and Oxford. The suggestion of homosexuality didn't unduly trouble him. Young men went through the phase sometimes and emerged to become perfectly satisfactory husbands and fathers, and Arthur, he knew for a fact, had had, in the past, a good share of sultry affairs with women, mostly those of a lower order who could be dismissed after the pleasurable interludes, leaving no undue pangs of conscience behind. So he wasn't without passion, thank God. But what kind? And what had he done so soon to cause a rift between him and Emma?

Oh yes. The more he brooded on things when he had time, the more certain Jonathan was that there'd been a misunderstanding of some kind.

He tried probing Jessie's mind, subtly at first, then when she didn't respond, more bluntly.

'Do *you* think Arthur and Emma get on all right?' he asked one day. 'Is there something wrong between them?'

Jessie shrugged. 'How should I know? Emma's not my kind, she doesn't confide in me. She finds me boring, I suppose. I'm not interested in being glamorous, or charming businessmen, or having my name at the head of a newspaper column. Why don't you ask *her*? She might say. Or Arthur.' She looked away, knowing Arthur was the last person his father would tackle, simply because he wouldn't get an honest reply.

Jonathan grunted.

'You're not much help. And you should be. Women are supposed to have insight into these things.'

'Then why don't you speak to Mama?' Jessie's eyes held a momentary gleam of mischief that for a brief few seconds made her plain face almost attractive.

Jonathan turned and saying nothing more, strode down the

hall irritably and out of the front door. Speak to his wife! The very idea! — when her sole concern was to paint her ageing kittenish face, see that cook attended to the menus adequately, retiring later for a siesta with her glass of tonic or Madeira.

All the same, that same evening he made one of his rare visits to his wife's room. She was seated before her gilt-framed dressing-table mirror, patting her plump cheeks with cream. Her yellow hair, still thick for a woman of her age, fell about her spreading white shoulders. She was wearing a negligée over her nightdress of pale pink georgette.

She turned when the door opened, and to a man of finer sensibilities her look of pleasure and gratification would have aroused a touch of sympathy. He felt only irritation, knowing that he'd have to endure a tiresome session — however short — of lovemaking, before he got anything out of her that might cast aspersion on the character of her pampered beloved son.

'Hm!' he cleared his throat. 'You're looking very — fetching,' he lied, going towards her.

She got up, one hand pressed to a plump breast. Why on earth didn't she diet? he wondered. She was becoming almost gross in size, and though her flesh was white enough, and her skin good, there was far too much of it.

'Oh Jonathan,' she gushed, 'it's right good to have thee here.' She paused before adding, 'Is everything all right, love?'

He closed his eyes and let his lips touch her shoulder. It was fragrant and soft. Without looking at her he could almost imagine her as the girl he'd seduced so long ago.

After that, the passionate ritual was simple, and not half so distasteful as he'd imagined. When they lay afterwards side by side on the ornate bed, he started his subtle inquisition.

Amelia, though a simple woman in many ways, glanced at him warily. There were certain aspects of his character she knew well, and when Jonathan approached her over any subject in that devious particular way — over-casually, yet with subtle flattering innuendoes in his voice and manner, she recognised he was up to something. Something in which she could be useful. So that was it! He'd wanted her not for herself that night, as she'd foolishly imagined, but for what he could get out of her. Disillusion gripped her for a moment, then she smothered it with her usual commonsense. It was something, after all, that he depended on her for anything these days, coming to her bed whatever the reason might be.

'—As a mother and a woman—' he was saying, 'you've got a knowledge over certain matters I don't have. Maybe we've not seemed so close lately as we could've been. But I'm a busy man, and you've got enough on your hands taking care of this establishment without being burdened by my affairs.'

'I do what I can, Jonathan,' she said primly.

'Yes. Well—' He touched a stout forearm intimately and sensing the hidden response in her that she managed not to show, continued bluntly, 'It's Arthur.'

'*Arthur?*' She was surprised.

He attempted to explain his doubts of Bradley junior's relationship to Emma, and found it more difficult than he'd imagined, simply because he'd nothing tangible to go on.

Amelia shook her head slowly. 'They sleep together,' she said. 'They don't quarrel that I know of. What makes thee suspicious? I've noticed naught—'

'I know. That's part of it. There's nothing *to* notice, except that Emma's so restless and always poking her head into business affairs. She's a *damned* nuisance, and I thought you might be able to find out why. Get her talking; discover why she doesn't spend more time here, at Eastwood. Has she thought of starting a family? – That sort of thing.'

'I'll try,' Amelia answered doubtfully. 'But Emma and me – we're not exactly close. She avoids me as much as she can, thinks me a meddlesome old bore, I reckon.' A low chuckle escaped her, 'And she's probably right. If she was a bit interested in the home, love, it'd be different. But she's not. It's all the paper and getting to Oaklands to see that poor little sister of hers – Rosalind. Maybe if it wasn't for her she'd be thinking of a child of her own. But time's short yet. Don't worry. Young women these days like a bit of freedom afore startin' with nappies and sleepless nights. It'll all work out. And once the Dower House business is settled she'll find more'n enough to occupy her without treading on *your* toes. Anyway, Arthur wouldn't want her dangling round his neck all day. He's a bit of a loner, you know — a rum one in his way. And if it pleases Emma to bother about the *Echo* why should it worry *thee* so much?'

'It's important,' Jonathan answered abruptly. 'I've been a fool in allowing her so much power. I shouldn't have listened to Arthur. But he was so besotted — and apparently it was a condition—'

'A *condition*?'

'If she wed him, Oaklands and the paper had to remain independent — of me.'

'Of *you*? You mean you let her dictate?'

'To *him*? Yes. I thought marriage might steady him, bring him down to earth. So I gave in. But it hasn't affected him in the right way at all. He spends an hour or so a day at Feyland, with the *Comet* — studying accounts, throwing a few fine suggestions and orders about, then back again to the stables and horses. At board meetings he supports me, though I don't think he cares a bloody damn about business really.'

'With his background does he have to?'

'Don't be a fool, Amelia.' She winced. 'When election time comes round I shall need intelligent backing and help — especially from the press, and my family. At the moment it looks as though I'll have to fight for it. Especially with the young madam Arthur's married against me.'

'*Emma? Against* you?'

'And don't echo what I say, woman.' He got up, swung himself out of bed quickly and reached for his shirt. 'She's already started — by getting that fiery Welshman, Evan Lloyd, nominated as editor of the *Echo*.'

After a pause, Amelia dared to ask meekly, 'Is there anything against him being Welsh, Jonathan?'

He didn't reply, merely grabbed the rest of his clothes, dressed and left her, slamming the door sharply behind him.

She sighed, lay for a few moments in heavy disappointment, then reached for her own particular brand of tonic.

Jonathan meanwhile went to his study, perused documents, figures and studied recent editions of the rival Feyland *Courier*, after which he indulged himself with two glasses of vintage brandy before taking a short stroll about the grounds. The liquor dimmed his dark mood. It was a fine night, with a rising moon in the sky.

He'd get there, by God, he told himself, by the time the next election was over he'd have won his seat in the House, Emma or no Emma.

Aye! And somehow he'd find a way of bringing that son of his to heel. He'd be on to him like a leech from now on; and if he found his son and heir up to any little abnormal sexual games he'd have the hide off his back or disinherit him. Until then he hadn't frankly admitted his suspicions, even to himself. But the fact had to be faced sometime. Arthur, in some curious subtle way, was perverted, and had to be brought to a normal way of behaviour before the county knew.

His whole future could depend on this. There must be proof that besides the Bradley millions the family was capable of founding a strong and healthy dynasty. Therefore Emma and his son must produce an heir. Not for the first time he wished fervently that Arthur had only waited — held his horses until a more suitable match could be arranged. There were plenty of good-looking young women around, and Leyfordshire was noted for its pretty girls. In another couple of years, with luck, the Bradleys would have become accepted in the county — recognised as a power and asset to the community. Already he and his son were members of the Quayle Hunt; furthermore Jonathan was nibbling for an invitation to join a certain select club that would establish him firmly in the eyes of the majority of members. A few toffee-nosed snobs might cold-shoulder him — at the beginning. But Lord Wendle was on his side, and could be persuaded, through subtle means, Jonathan sensed, to back him as prospective Conservative candidate for East Leyfordshire. Wendle himself was a bit of an anachronism. But this was one of the strange things he had discovered, about the local aristocracy. True blue-bloods could afford to be democratic, whereas half-way socialities still had to keep a rigid eye on the climbers' ladder. And, of course, finance came into it. Wendle was always in need of cash. And there Jonathan Bradley held the whip hand.

Neither man had any illusions abut the other's aims or ambitions. This in itself held a camaraderie between them that was not only useful, but refreshing. Wendle was a good-humoured sporty old boy, Jonathan told himself frequently, and it was a pity his only daughter, Leila, hadn't been better-looking. A union between the two families could have been advantageous to both. But Leila Wendle was the large, hearty, fox-hunting type — good in the saddle, and with a gusty sense of humour. But there her assets ended. As a wife for Arthur her chances from the beginning had been nil.

Damn it all though, why on earth had Emma appeared on the scene just at the crucially wrong moment? And now she had, why couldn't she do her duty, keep Arthur more in tow, and produce the heir so desperately needed? A child was the only answer — someone to keep her chained to the home instead of interfering with the *Echo*.

The next day he made a point of following her when she went into the conservatory for flowers for the house. Since Amelia seemed so half-hearted about the subject, he'd decided on a direct approach.

She was snipping at a spray of scarlet blooms — some exotic foreign variety — as he strode in.

'Ah!' he said with forced cheer in his voice, 'warm in here, isn't it? And decorative. What are those things called, do you know? The late owner, Billington his name was, or something like it, had travelled a good deal. An authority on flowers and strange plants.'

To his surprise Emma knew the answer.

'Of course,' he said, recollecting her nature campaign in the *Echo*. 'I suppose you've had to do a good bit of reading up about these things to please your public. The sort of subject that goes down well with women.'

He waited for her reaction, but when she glanced at him

briefly, her face was expressionless yet discerning. Then she turned to give another snap of her scissors.

'Oh I don't deal with foreign flowers for the paper,' she said casually. 'It wouldn't be at all popular. Most women have a creative streak in them; it's a matter of how to draw it out — and for that you have to have an everyday basis — something that costs nothing preferably. I mean it's generally only rich people who have conservatories. So what would be the point of giving hints on flower arrangement if you use tropical blossoms and plants? Besides, autumn leaves, grasses — even certain twigs, can look lovely, and don't cost a penny.'

'I see,' Jonathan said stiffly, with the uncomfortable feeling of having been subtly put in his place. 'But once you've said that, it's done with, isn't it? You can't keep on repeating how to arrange autumn leaves and berries.'

A hint of mischief lit Emma's eyes. 'Oh, but I don't, Mr Bradley. Which you'd know, if you read my articles.' She laid the scissors down and rubbed her hands on the dainty apron she was wearing. Then she pulled the frilly thing off and laid it on a seat. There was a smile on her face when she asked, 'But you didn't follow me here to talk of botany, did you?'

'No,' he said bluntly, 'and I wish you wouldn't call me "Mr Bradley". Say "Jonathan" if you like — I don't care. Or else "pater". I'm "pater" or "the old man" to Arthur, and I prefer the first. Infernally snobbish, but that's what Oxford does, and as his wife you'd better follow suit.'

'All right — Pater.'

'You know what it means, of course — father of the house — I realise I don't have to tell you, being the intellectual young woman you are.'

'No,' she still looked slightly roguish. 'I *have* heard of it.'

'Well, then!' Jonathan gave a sigh before resuming. 'When you two have children of your own it'll be "grandfather" I suppose, or else "grandaddy". I'm looking forward to that day, Emma. Do you and Arthur ever discuss it?'

There was quite a pause before Emma answered. 'We haven't been married very long, and Arthur has had horses very much on his mind. As you know he pops off to Newmarket quite a lot these days, and when we *do* discuss the future it's mostly about the Dower House.'

'Yes, I suppose so. You'll have a lot to think about there. And that's natural. The right thing to do; I'm sure of it now. A newly married couple need an independent starting-home. A nest for the future you could say. There'll not be so much time for you to be running off to Oaklands.'

'Oaklands seems to worry you,' Emma said. 'You resent it, don't you?'

'My dear girl, the place doesn't affect me one way or the other,' Jonathan bluffed. 'Except—'

'Yes?'

'It can be an excuse for going to Charbrook,' he told her. 'When I — or rather when Arthur made it possible to have the *Echo* still under your pretty little thumb — neither of us realised quite how powerfully you meant to use it.'

She laughed.

'You exaggerate. I've missed one or two board meetings already. I only want to — to keep *certain* characteristics of the paper as they've always been. I suppose out of respect — memory of my father.'

'The true naive little sentimentalist.' His voice was wry.

She gave him a very direct look, and at that moment, before she said, 'You could call me that I suppose in some ways—' he was aware that his statement was indeed true. 'Naive' might have been the wrong word to use, but the clarity of her very clear grey eyes indicated an innocence and purity of purpose quite astonishing to his acute business sense. It was this quality in her that defeated his understanding. Whatever problem Arthur Bradley might present, his devious off-course attitude to life was of the worldly order. Beneath his brilliant handsome facade, a twisted streak glimmered unpleasantly at odd moments. Jonathan so far had managed mostly to disregard it. But he knew now, uncomfortably, that this girl never would. Her integrity — to whatever cause, however mistakenly — would endure to the bitter conclusion of any conflict. She was as stubborn in her own way as that Welsh rebel, Evan Lloyd, whom she'd successully wheedled or forced into the *Echo*'s orbit.

Remembering Evan temporarily swept other matters aside. The man had been accepted and was taking over the editorship the following week. There'd be a whole introductory article from him, he supposed irritably; he only hoped Lloyd would keep it on as low and practical a key as possible. No doubt his photograph would be displayed. The fellow had a good head, and impudent swaggering profile.

'Quite — powerful looking,' Emma had observed regarding the portrait at the last office meeting. 'I think he'll go down well.'

Jonathan had grunted. He wasn't so sure, but he'd a shrewd idea the women would be impressed, and that when Evan set his mind to a project he'd be justly dogged about it.

Well, the point now was that somehow he had to be brought round to presenting and supporting certain of Jonathan's own views. Politically especially. The *Echo* might be a small paper, but its influence could disrupt the power of the *Comet* to a certain extent, and be a cog in the wheel of the founding of *The Midlander*. This mustn't happen. Somehow or other he'd win Evan round. If he didn't, the man would go, and so would the paper itself, he'd see to that. Emma might hold the ruling shares, but without the other half, the *Echo* could never endure; it was within his — Jonathan's — capacity to close down, should the absolute necessity arise.

As though sensing his travel of thought, Emma said, 'You didn't *really* want to talk about newspapers just now, did you? It was to tell me how you wanted Arthur and me to have a baby.'

'Both. As I've only one son to inherit all I've worked for — and damned hard, let me tell you — I naturally want the family line to endure. In the normal way there'd have been no question of it, but—'

'As he's married an abnormal woman you're worried,' Emma interrupted sharply.

He paused before he spoke. She could feel his eyes burning into hers, searching through every curve of her enticing young body to the hidden impulses and motivations that made her what she was — exciting and damned attractive to the male libido, but at the same time inaccessible and remote, a contradiction with subleties in her which could be exceedingly irritating.

No wonder Arthur had wanted her. She was a challenge; all the same some wealthy young brood mare would have fitted far better into the scheme of things. She could feel her colour deepening, as he said, 'There's nothing abnormal about *you*, Emma. But as we're speaking plainly, I'll be frank. I didn't approve the marriage. Arthur had far better chances socially, and you're too intellectual to fit easily into our way of life. I can understand him being intrigued though — you too. You didn't marry a nobody, did you? He had damn good looks that'd sweep most girls off their feet, and loaded into the bargain.'

'With money you mean.' Her voice was faintly contemptuous.

'Yes. Money. The money that saved your precious *Echo*. Well—' his jaw took a pugnacious thrust '—I'm not grudging it, providing you play fair, keep to your proper place, and see my son gives you a child. Understand?'

Her cheeks had paled.

'Perfectly. But remember two are concerned in such a project.'

'Now what the devil—' He didn't finish. Emma had turned her back on him and was arranging the sprays of blooms in a small basket on her arm. He sighed, and walked heavily to the inner door, only pausing to say, before leaving, 'Think over what I've said. It's important.'

She knew it was, and in a desperate moment of clarity recognised also how badly she'd failed in assessing Arthur's character. What was it he wanted of her? Not love, certainly. Submission? Yes, probably. An heir? She doubted it. He wasn't interested in children and during the first weeks of marriage had effectively put her off wishing for any of his. Yet at the beginning he'd charmed her by being flattering and courteous. She'd believed that, emotionally, beneath his elegant facade he was a normal man, with the underlying instincts to make an enduring relationship of their marriage.

Well, she'd been wrong.

He wasn't.

Her only hope was in some way to salvage a basic friendship from the union. The thought was sterile, bitter, and it didn't help knowing how disappointed her father-in-law was going to be in the future.

That evening, Arthur, sensing an extra quietness and withdrawal in her, was sufficiently intrigued to ask curiously, 'What are you milling over, gorgeous?'

She was sitting at her dressing table, brushing the thick shining masses of chestnut-dark hair. No — not chestnut, he thought critically, copper-beech, that was it — a colour that changed subtly every time a beam of light caught it. He had an impulse to run his hand through it, twist it round her lovely neck gently, then draw it to his lips.

At the first mere touch of his hand she stiffened, 'Oh don't, Arthur. You'll tangle it.'

She shook it free, and his fingers enclosed her shoulder. They were very strong, and hurt. She looked up at him; his blue eyes blazed down on her as though lit by white fire.

'Aren't I allowed to touch my own wife?'

'*Wife?*' she echoed. 'Did you say "wife", Arthur?'

'What the devil do you mean?'

'You know very well.' She paused before adding, 'Or perhaps you don't. Perhaps you just wanted me as a — a kind of curiosity, because I'm different and didn't run after you. *A specimen.*'

He laughed, released her, and pushed her on to the bed. She fell back but recovered herself swiftly and sat up.

'Stay there,' he remarked, taking out his handkerchief and wiping his brow. 'You do as I say and we'll be all right. A specimen, possession — call it what you like. It's not an insult. If you hadn't been so intriguing I wouldn't have looked at you. I'm — a connoisseur, shall we say? I don't care for ordinary human beings or situations. It's the unusual I go for. The unique; and you're certainly that, Emma.' His voice trembled slightly, but his eyes remained hard and shining. His expression disturbed her. She edged back; he caught her by the neck of her night-dress and pulled her forward. 'Frightened, darling? You needn't be. Provided you behave. If you don't, I have that handy little whip of mine. Some women like being thrashed. Do you, Emma?'

She jerked herself free and rushed to the other side of the bed. Breathing heavily, she gasped, '—If you touch me, Arthur Bradley, I'll − I'll—'

He smiled. 'Well? What will you do? Run away? Tell my esteemed Papa? Divorce me? But you can't, my love, as I said − a man's *allowed* to touch his wife. So—' his voice hardened, 'come here instantly. You needn't be afraid. There'll be no whipping − yet; no scenes, no crying or shrieking for help. Just a little − tuition, sweetheart. In the methods of loving. You want to be loved, don't you? Then let me teach you.'

She didn't move.

'No.'

'Very well.' He strode towards her, and pulled the nightdress from her body letting it fall and lie in a crumpled heap at her feet. Rigid, but inwardly trembling, she stood pale and naked before him, yet with her swift mind already concentrating on a nearby heavy candlestick which she meant to spring for, if he attacked her.

But there was no need; with his blue eyes half closed, he touched first one soft breast, before his hand travelled insidiously, half consciously down her side to the gentle swelling of thigh and buttocks. Then he knelt down and kissed her bare toes. Involuntarily she shivered. He looked up, and she was astonished to see the glint of tears in his blue eyes.

'So beautiful,' he murmured thickly, 'so innocent and pure − pure as a young boy, as David—'

'David?'

'My friend.' The simple statement stunned her temporarily, until she said, 'I don't understand.' But somewhere, dark at the back of her mind, she did.

'Forgive me,' he said, reaching for her hand. 'Forgive me for being different and for wanting — the impossible. I *do* want you, you know, Emma — but not in *your* way. No children. No scheming sentimental preliminaries. In time, when you've become adjusted—'

She made a sudden violent movement, reached for her wrap, and pulled it round her fiercely. 'You're mad, Arthur,' she said coldly and very clearly, 'and don't ever dare to approach me again, or I'll tell your father — everything. Yes, I will, and he'll disinherit you.'

Rage rose in him again with a violence that drove her to the door.

'If you do that,' he said, 'I'll kill you, and I mean it. Or—' his lips twisted wrily into a mad semblance of a smile as he forced himself to be more calm, 'maybe I'd just inform him what a cheat and liar you are. There are ways you know — the countryside's not short of some stupid little whore in the family way — isn't that what they call it? — who could be easily paid, and proud to name *me* as their bastard's wicked papa — where would you be then, Emma, my love? Out in the cold, a frigid wife drawing him to another woman, and therefore no longer a member of the Bradley family. *I'd* see you soon lost your Oaklands and your precious *Echo* — I was cunning enough to have a clause inserted in the agreement which *does* give me a certain power.'

'I don't believe you.'

'You'd better. And now—' astonishingly he held out a conciliatory hand, 'let us be friends, shall we? Possibly, in time, you may learn to co-operate concerning our connubial existence. We could have fun, you know—'

'*Fun!*' Her voice was vituperative with contempt. 'I *hate* you.'

He shrugged. 'Oh well — that's a beginning.'

'Do you mind going.'

'Not at all.'

He left. And when the latch had clicked a wave of dizziness swept over her. She stood for a moment, until her head had cleared, then staggered to the window, pushed it open, and let the cool spring wind brush the darkness from her eyes.

The following week she had an interview with Evan Lloyd.

6

They sat facing each other at a small table where two cups of coffee were placed, with a conglomeration of files, newspaper cuttings, and other papers pushed to one side. The larger table across the window appeared in worse confusion; documents and letters everywhere — rather similar to an illustration from *Alice-in-Wonderland*, Emma thought, wondering how on earth any human being would manage to get it into order. She had been there once or twice before during her father's day. It had been a bit of a jumble then — but discreetly so, with glory holes, as William had called them, giving a facade of normality and order.

'There aren't proper places to keep the things in,' he'd explained. 'And if a sub-editor's off, or on calls, I have the whole lot to deal with myself. Now, Emma—' and he'd wagged a finger at her, 'don't tell me you're all tidy yourself—' and she'd laughed, remembering her wardrobe and chest-of-drawers at Oaklands where so many feminine fripperies, blouses, and underwear were often to be found, after a search, in the one place where they shouldn't be.

Still — *this*!

Her eyes, after wandering briefly round the littered floor and desk, came back to Evan who was watching her expectantly, with a whimsical lop-sided smile on his mouth.

'Pretty awful, isn't it,' he said. 'I shall get things sorted out in time, and the quicker the better, so I can start making my own muddles.'

'Oh. I see.' Although she didn't.

He watched her intently. The pause between them was electric, filled with an astonishment, a magic that was new to

her, and profoundly disturbing. Lloyd was not handsome in the
conventional style of Arthur − his features had a rebellious yet
Puckish quality expressing a man capable of many moods,
wayward perhaps, and with an impudent sense of humour, yet
strong and purposeful. He had a slightly tilted nose above well-
sculpted lips and a dogged cleft chin. His eyes were light and
sparkling, varying between green and grey; his hair brown,
curling rebelliously from a wide intellectual forehead. Yes.
There was certainly something magnetic about him that set
Emma's spine tingling. For this reason she appeared aloof, a
little chilly.

When she said no more he continued, in casual, almost
offhand tones, 'Newspapers aren't produced in ladies' drawing
rooms, as you should know, Miss Fairley—' he corrected himself
quickly, '—sorry. Mrs Bradley. The end product has to be in
order, but getting the order means sometimes a darn lot of
searching, sorting and puzzling out. Journalists − including
editors − have all their own individual systems and aims. Mine
may be very different to your father's. We shall see.'

'I hope not *too* different,' she said sharply.

His eyes once more flung her a quick quizzical glance. The
next question was blunt and sudden, taking her unawares.

'*Why* have you come to see me today, Emma? Yes, if you
don't mind I shall call you Emma right away, because if you
continue with your column − which I hope you will − you'll be a
member of my staff, and formalities won't be necessary.'

'All right.' An involuntary smile puckered her pretty lips. 'In
that case you'll be Evan to me. Correct?'

He shook his head. '*No*. Most *in*correct. At Board meetings
and in public you can address me as Mr Lloyd, but in private it
should certainly be "Sir". Don't you agree?'

She frowned, wondering if he was joking, and suddenly he
laughed; he *was*. 'For goodness sake,' he said, and his voice held
a Welsh lilt in it, 'don't look like that—' The humour in his eyes
faded, as he noted − with a rush of deepening interest tinged
with something else, something more personal than admiration; more restrained than physical desire − the glowing

colour mount her beautifully modelled cheeks, the proud set of her small head on the slim neck, exquisite features and russet curls straying below the brim of her absurd little velvet hat.

'Like what?' she asked, with her heart pumping at her throat.

He looked at a paper. 'I think I know. Being Welsh — a bit of scribbler-poet, I'm apt to let my imagination stray. I could say, I suppose, "a wild deer in a cool green forest — an elusive creature as swift and intrinsically gentle as the wayward winds of spring". On the other hand it could just as well be — "an attractive inquisitive girl wanting to poke her nose into other people's business".'

'Thank you *very* much.'

'Don't mention it. So long as we know where we stand, maybe it's time we got down to brass tacks, meaning, of course, our little business tête-a-tête.'

Although her mind and senses were still reeling, she managed to say, while fiddling with a froth of white lace edging the high neck of her waisted green velvet jacket, 'Yes, high time.'

Their following discussion, concerning the layout of the *Echo*, was surprisingly easy. Lloyd's ideas she discovered were flexible and mostly in harmony with her own. He wanted very little change, but suggested she should have a whole page, temporarily anyway, for social and feminine affairs, with space allotted also for any serious article she wished to deal with.

Of course she wished it. It was what she'd argued over with her father constantly.

'You'd have to talk over any — revolutionary idea with me first, of course,' he said over-casually, 'and I take it you'd be free of domestic ties to do it.'

Her back stiffened, giving her chin a higher tilt.

'Of course,' she said very clearly. 'My duties at Eastwood aren't many. In fact, I'm not needed in that way at all, really.'

He tore his eyes away from hers with difficulty. She'd appeared in that flash of time so vulnerable, and almost hurt, beneath the bravado and facade of independence.

'Then that's fine. It's settled. I'd suggest, though, we hold our horses temporarily over the additional stuff — the articles. You'll have to do me a specimen copy, anyway.'

'Naturally.' She got up, and he was inwardly amused to note the touch of defiance in her very erect pose, the almost discernible upthrust of young breasts beneath the fitted velvet jacket. 'My father never complained about my writing,' she added, 'and he was a good critic. His reviews went quite far afield, you know; even *The Stage* asked for them when any important show came to the Charbrook Olympia. He wrote up Ellen Terry in—'

'I know, I know,' Evan interrupted, waving a hand. 'I don't need reminding of William Fairley's prowess, and I'm sure I shan't have to complain about yours. But dramatic reviewing's very different from driving a strong point home in as few words as possible. That needs punch, fire, and enthusiasm. Also ability. The art of coming to the point quickly and firing the public conscience. Dash! drive! — so that controversy's roused. Do you understand?'

The light in his eyes had swept away hurt pride in her by a rush of enthusiasm.

'Yes. Of course I do.'

He took her hand then; its warm pressure thrilled her whole being. As their eyes met once more, expectancy, excitement, and a sense of overwhelming delight flowered between them.

In a dazed moment she heard him say, 'What a pity you're married, Emma Fairley, I should like to kiss you.'

The tips of two pearly teeth glimmered between her parted lips, as she said, half whispering, 'You can, if you like.'

His mouth was firm but gentle as it came down briefly upon hers. The contact was soon over, but she felt joyous, revitalised, when a moment later he showed her to the door.

Outside the Charbrook streets were patterned by the transient light and shade of the spring afternoon; ordinary streets of ordinary houes, with pedestrians, shoppers mostly, about their daily routine. Yet to her, the whole world seemed suddenly to be singing. In the last hour life had become different, completely changed for her.

That was how it began

*

During the next few days following the revealing and unpredictable emotional impact of her meeting with Lloyd, Emma was
careful at Eastwood to control her suddenly awakened delight
under a veneer of pleasant calm which did not entirely deceive
Arthur. Where, before, she had frequently responded to his
annoying manner of teasing, by quick-tempered rejoinders
which he delighted in quelling, she now accepted with apparent
unruffled calm. She tried not to betray dislike when his hand
touched her body possessively. But he sensed that any hope or
longing in her for a consummated relationship between them,
had now faded into acquiescence of a completely sterile role.
She would not accept his pleasurable indulgencies. She desired
him to be *ordinary* — behave like any other conventional,
normally sexed husband. Before, this wouldn't have troubled
him, but he was puzzled by the secret glow about her which at
times brought a meditative smile to her lips, and a shining
translucent light to her eyes. He was annoyed too, because he
knew very well it did not concern him. There was nothing he
could put his finger on; but the fact that she had in any way the
capacity to elude him irritated him to deepening sullen anger.
She was his after all. He'd married her — she belonged. And by
God if he caught her out in any funny business he'd take the
whip to her back.

In the meantime he took it out on his dogs and horses — all
except Thunder, his chestnut stallion whose blazing tawny eyes,
magnificent frame, waving mane and pounding hooves were a
match any day for his own wild thwarted spirit. There was
affinity between them; they were, in a sense, counterparts of
different species in all but one thing. Thunder could sire strong
specimens of his kind. He, Arthur Bradley, could not. Neither
did he wish to — only to possess — in any warped erratic way he
fancied. And so far he hadn't abused his rights over Emma,
merely deprived her.

Where had it all begun? Wherein was the origin of his

abnormality? What twisted gene had driven him, in early youth, to find active pleasure only through his own sex or in sadistic lust? Did his father know? Was he even aware of it? He doubted it, although occasionally he'd caught an assessing, half-bewildered glance in Jonathan's eyes. Arthur then, had felt more than ever irritated; why hadn't Bradley senior given his mother more sons? It was as though, having bred one outwardly perfect physical specimen, and following the birth of Jessie a boring, plain daughter, he'd given up, to concentrate all his hopes and future plans on Arthur.

Well, if that was so — if it was expected of him and Emma to found a dynasty, the old man was going to be disappointed.

The one redeeming fact, to Arthur, about the situation, was that the intriguing and lovely Emma was no longer free to produce others in her image. She was his alone, and he'd see she remained so.

7

Young summer came to the forest, sprinkling the valleys with carpets of bluebells glimmering in massed patches between the trees. Through pale trunks of silver birch and tender green leaves of oak and sycamore, the deep shining tarns of Feyland Woods shone deeply mysterious, broodingly dark one moment, the next dappled in transient sunlight to ever-changing ripples of purple and jade blue, lit to gold. There was a magical, almost legendary quality about the area that was nevertheless dangerous to strangers and the unwary. At points attempts had been made to fence certain places, but of the four pools only one was properly protected. The largest, nick-named locally as Green Harry, had been the scene in the past of several fatal accidents − including a horse and cart that had blundered off the track one misty night, and taken a farmer to his death. Also more than one suicide of which only a single body had been recovered. So alongside beauty lingered a sinister quality, giving the woods a reputation for being haunted.

Emma, however, from being a child had always loved the vicinity, which was only a mile or two from Bradgate and not far, as the crow flies, from Oaklands. She knew every secret path winding through thick tall bracken, past lush pale green dells, hoping, but not really believing, that one day she might catch a glimpse of the ill-fated Lady Jane Grey's ghost gliding through shadowed branches, damp with rising mist. To most people the story was merely imagination, but many locals stressed its truth.

Emma did not actually believe in visual ghosts but having lived so close to nature she was aware of strange influences and sometimes unexplainable happenings that could not be described in material terms. The sensitivity that had responded so immediately to Evan Lloyd had an instinctive affinity with moods of the unseen. Rosalind, too, though deprived of normal reasoning, had a deep, or as Emma termed, 'other knowledge' in her, which felt the same intuitive fascination. Places affected her more than people. Often, during her short life, she had beguiled Emma into taking her to the tarns, where she'd stand entranced, like some beautiful changeling creature, staring into the brooding azure depths.

Emma had watched her, saddened by the pathetic loveliness which would never know the normal fulfilment of a woman, wondering what thoughts, if any, haunted the little girl's bewildered hidden mind. Rosalind seldom gave indication that she had any, although she could say a few words indicating when she was hungry or wanted the toilet. Animals and birds seemed to have unconscious affinity with her. They were never afraid when she approached, and the child would smile then, an elfin far-away smile, holding out a pale hand so a tit, sparrow, or robin would perch there. Even a nearby farmer's dog that had been taught to be surly and bark shrilly, was quiet and gentle with her, wagging its tail and pushing its shaggy face up to be patted when it saw her. Emma's affection for her she simply accepted as a right — but was quite happy without it, and although generally docile, she had occasional tempers when thwarted, which died as quickly as a current of wind gone suddenly quiet.

Following Emma's departure to Eastwood, the housekeeper had developed quite a fierce pride in the little girl's beauty, and although the governess-nurse was nominally in charge of her, the older woman saw to it that she had prior command and kept a watchful eye on daily life at Oaklands.

'She misses you though,' she told Emma one summer day when she called. 'Oh yes. She has more depths in her than you think.'

Emma shook her head, smiling sadly. 'No, Mrs Cox, I'm sure that's not true. And I wouldn't want it to be. How could I be happy at all away from here, if I thought Rosalind was suffering for it?'

'Young women in love can be happy anywhere if the lover's there too,' came the answer a trifle sharply, and Emma for a quick second or two felt a guilty wave of joy surge through her. Was her potential happiness so obvious? So obvious that anyone could remotely guess the completely unexpected development her emotional life had taken? Evan? But no. They had met only once since that first interview alone together at Charbrook, and members of the board, including Arthur who was seldom present, had been there. Both Evan and Emma had been careful to give no indication of their inner feelings, had each even managed to avoid direct conversation with the other. But the electrical awareness had been there. Once when she'd caught a fleeting glance of his eyes upon her, her whole body had thrilled and stiffened, leaving, as she'd managed to look away, a swooning sense of delight in her.

Nobody could have noticed, she was sure. But later Arthur had said, 'That fellow, Lloyd. I don't like him.'

'Oh?' Her tone was impersonal, disinterested.

'He's a revolutionary.'

'Don't be ridiculous.'

'I know the type.'

'And I'm quite sure he knows yours,' she'd thought, but mercifully had controlled herself sufficiently to make no response.

Now, on this particular afternoon, with Eastwood miles away, and the sweetly-sad nostalgic sighing of the woods about her, Emma felt an irresistible desire to have a glimpse, face to face, of the man who'd awakened such wild emotions in her. Under the genuine pretext of making a visit to Rosalind there'd been a secret hope that she might come across him by chance, either down one of the lanes, in his car, or perhaps on foot. The latter was unlikely, of course. During the week Lloyd was mostly confined to his office, working hectically, as the following morning was publishing day for the weekly. Thinking briefly about her own column, she realised it wasn't quite up to standard, the reason being her own emotional involvement with personal matters. She'd have to pull herself together or he might not want her work at all. The prospect of special articles would fade, and with it many chances of meeting him.

That mustn't happen.

And with her decision came another. She *must* see him that very day and explain. He'd understand. He felt the same way about her, as she of him, only in his case, of course, being a man made him more capable of keeping business matters completely apart from the romantic.

Still – a fleeting smile touched her lips; just for a few precious moments she could surely penetrate officialdom.

Because of the sudden urgency in her, her walk with Rosalind was short that day. They wandered hand-in-hand, picking a few wild flowers and ferns, while Emma hummed an old tune from childhood days that somehow captured the atmosphere of place. Occasionally Rosalind's light voice joined in. Looking down into the lovely upturned young face, Emma was filled with regret because the luminous dark-fringed eyes, though momentarily happy, were completely devoid of understanding, reflecting only an awareness of elemental instinctive forces. The sun on her flaxen hair felt good. It was nice to hear the chortle of birds and feel the soft grass brush her legs. Otherwise the world was empty of meaning, and would be, Emma sensed, for always. Rosalind would never know how to reason, never savour the ache and longing for a home, lover and husband. When she was older, being so beautiful, men might desire her, and through that she would be in danger. It would be hers – Emma's duty – to see she was protected from assault and despoilment.

However, that problem was for the future, and mustn't destroy any joy of the present.

When the time came to return to Oaklands, Rosalind was acquiescent, though her pretty underlip pouted.

'Tarn?' she murmured questioningly. 'Emma – tarn?'

'Not today, darling. Emma has work to do.'

'Work,' she thought as the little girl reluctantly accompanied her back. 'What a liar you are, Emma Fairley.' In her own mind she had already replaced the newly acquired 'Bradley' for her

father's name. Life at Eastwood was becoming increasingly
more distasteful to her.

By four o'clock she had joined the main road to Charbrook,
and in another twenty minutes was there.

8

The *Echo* offices stood in a side road of the town, near the canal,
and a railway yard adjoining a dye-works. As she approached
the steamy smell of water mingling faintly with that of newsprint rose in a wave of nostalgia to greet her — a familiarity
based on former days during her father's lifetime. Any wind
there'd been that afternoon had died, intensifying the damp
rising heat. The clip clop of horses' hooves and jingling of
harness came from the yard where the great shire horses ended
their day's toil. There was occasional shouting from a coal barge
drifting on the dark water towards the bridge.

All so familiar somehow, yet charged with a new magic to
Emma whose pulses had already quickened alarmingly as she
pushed the door to the *Echo*'s premises and stepped inside. She
had a short flight of stairs to take before reaching a rather dark
corridor leading to the editorial departments and Lloyd's
room.

Before rapping sharply, she adjusted her hat and smoothed a
curl from her cheek. Was he in, she wondered? Oh, she did
hope so. If he wasn't — or was too rushed by the hectic business
of seeing the daily and weekly editions brought out to bother
about her, she'd feel not only disappointed but somehow painfully humiliated. She'd leave immediately, pretend she'd been
merely passing and had called by chance to discuss a light
matter of no immediate importance, and a second later be

gone. If that happened she'd have to wait — perhaps for ages — until *he* contacted *her*, which would be almost unbearable.

Lloyd was in, however, and after a brief pause called, 'Yes? Come in.' His voice sounded on edge, irritable.

Emma turned the door knob and entered. Had she been aware how very striking she looked — young and entrancing in a new gold and russet outfit, complete with bustle and small hat tilted intriguingly forward, she'd have recognised his gasp of astonishment as one, also, of admiration. The pause between them was only momentary. His warm eyes lit up. He got up from his stool and came towards her.

'Emma,' he said, 'oh — Emma.'

'Hullo,' her voice was soft, shy. She wondered if he'd kiss her, and if he did, how she'd react — pull away conventionally, or respond. The latter, she knew. And then — but her thoughts were racing too far ahead. She mustn't anticipate — not here, in her dead father's sanctum. He wouldn't judge her, but neither would he approve. However much she desired Evan — however unhappy she might be in her abnormal marriage it was too soon yet to break faith. She could amost sense William's presence in that dusty darkish interior — hear him saying, 'Take care, Emma, love. Don't jump your fences. Go steadily — you've a reputation to keep up, and Oaklands—' All imagination of course, but in essence true. So in a way she was relieved when after only a warm hand-clasp he pulled a rickety chair from under the table, and told her to sit down. She did. 'I hope I've not come at too busy a time,' she began with a rush. 'I've been to see Rosalind at Oaklands, and I thought I'd call — perhaps I shouldn't have, though. Perhaps—'

'No, you shouldn't.' His voice was serious, his expression blank. But as she got to her feet preparing to do her vanishing act, he laughed, and panic in her subsided. 'My dear girl, don't be ridiculous. Sit down again at once or I'll — now what will I do? I really don't know; you appear such an elegant untouchable young lady. I'd really hate to ruffle a hair of your pretty head.'

She relaxed. 'It wouldn't be easy. This hat has so many pins in it, it's stuck on like glue.'

They both grinned. Then he asked, 'How long can you stay? As you know, it's publishing day, and I won't be free for a couple of hours. But—'

'I can't stay at all, Evan,' she told him. 'And—' with a rush of honesty confessed '—I wasn't just passing. I – I wanted to see you, that's all.'

'And my God, I've wanted to see you,' he told her. 'You've been torture to me – on my mind ever since the last meeting. Emma—'

'Yes?'

'We'll have to talk some time. I take it you realise that?'

'Of course.'

'Not here, though, not now.'

'When?'

He laughed, but his eyes were serious, warm and compelling. 'Give me a chance. We'll puzzle it out – settle it somehow – somewhere. Not in this poky hole, but where I can see you as you really are, without the hatpins and frills and furbelows.'

'Oh. Don't you like this dress?'

'No. As a fashion-plate, yes. But it's not you, Emma Fairley.'

'Bradley,' she corrected him.

'Oh yes, more's the pity; especially as I've heard the fellow's quite a bounder.'

She turned her head away, and walked to the door hoping he couldn't see the deepening rose colour of shame in her cheeks.

He was after her in a second and pulled her round to face him. 'Tell me,' he said, with his jaw thrust out aggressively, 'does he ill-treat you?'

Her answer was a question, ambiguous.

'Do you think I'd allow *that*?'

'You might, for the sake of the *Echo* and Oaklands. But if it's true, and I find out, I'll wring his blasted neck, and that's a promise.'

Regaining composure, and knowing he meant it, she said,

'Don't worry, I'm not stupid, Evan, and Arthur's not really a forceful character. Just—'

'Bent, twisted.'

She shrugged. 'I really don't know what you'd call it. Anyway—' she forced a smile, 'we don't see much of each other. He's too concerned with his horses, and—'

'Other unspeakable pursuits. I know.'

She was silent for a moment, then with a veneer of calm, said, 'Please don't worry about me, there's no need. I can take care of myself, and Jonathan, my father-in-law, is quite considerate to me. Generous in a way.'

The meeting ended there, inconclusively.

Minutes later Emma was making her way to the point where she'd left her car. A passing youth had to help her to crank it up, and after several grunts and heaves it started off and was taking her by the shortest possible route back to Eastwood. Pedestrians stared as she passed, and only then did it occur to her, with a wave of humour, that she must appear rather ludicrous at the wheel of one of 'them new-fangled things', wearing her smart outfit in her new hat with its shred of veiling floating behind!

9

During the first months of the *Comet*'s appearance, the circulation of the *Courier* had declined slightly, but by the late summer of 1904 it had regained most of its lost readership. In the beginning the new paper's brightness, including a page devoted to humour, including cartoons on aspects of ordinary life, had offset its extreme conservatism which had been cunningly kept at a low level. *Apparently*. Gradually, however, the man-in-the-street — beguiled also by an additional sheet of excellent photography and sensational headlines — had sensed political undercurrents, which eventually had driven him back to take up again the more dependable long-established *Courier*. The fact had registered almost immediately with the newly formed board of Bradley's *Comet*, and the price was instantly dropped by a halfpenny a copy, which had again stimulated the battle between the two newspapers.

Jonathan's resolve somehow to acquire the rival daily by fair means or foul — preferably the former — once more made an offer to Hardy Wilton, whose family had started and owned the paper for generations. It was quite an excessive sum, and Jonathan had high hopes it would be accepted. But Wilton took only a week to decline it politely. The fact was that had Wilton needed, or even wished for financial aid for the *Courier*, he had only to contact a certain well-known national press to get all the necessary backing. The firm had been as anxious as Jonathan, at one time, to amalgamate the *Courier* into its own particular group. Leyford was a thriving place, already rich through its boot and shoe trade and hosiery. Population was increasing rapidly; in the future any successful newspaper was going to more than double or treble its circulation.

The tycoons knew it; so did Wilton. Therefore he stuck to his guns, and the *Courier* remained the most affluent and widely read privately owned paper in the county. An independent — free of political party.

Jonathan was chagrined by the refusal of his offer and concentrated all the more on using the *Echo* as a vehicle of newsprint publicity to gain his own ends.

So far it hadn't worked, and this fact he put down sourly to the presence of Evan Lloyd being at the editorial helm — and Emma.

One day, losing patience, he confronted her when she returned from Oaklands.

After calling her into the library he waved the latest edition of the weekly at her, and said, 'What do you think you're doing, girl? What's all this? Eh? Explain if you can.'

Emma's brows rose slightly above her grey eyes.

'What do you mean? I don't understand.'

He flung the edition on the table angrily, pointing to the front page. She noticed that his hand was shaking.

'I think you do. And so does he. You're in collusion, aren't you — you two?'

'Collusion?' Her voice held exasperation tinged with contempt. 'Why? *How?* — for goodness sake—'

'And don't "goodness sake" me, girl. You know the rules — you made enough show after your father died of wanting to keep the paper the way he liked it. I trusted you, so did Arthur. We made it possible to survive. But there were terms too, weren't there? Conditions. No politics, no changes offensive to the board and smaller shareholders. Well then — what do you think *that* is?' He waited for a second, breathing heavily before continuing, 'Breach of contract, pure and simple. I can sue that fellow Lloyd for this. Now — have you got facts into your head? Well think sharp and tell me what you're going to do about it.'

Emma studied the sheet before her. Its headlines below *Charbrook Echo* were — 'Challenge to Leyford Authorities'. And underneath, covering three columns — an outspoken article condemning the County Council for its political bigotry, and lack of feeling to the underprivileged and needy, especially where housing was concerned. After a tart outspoken beginning, the lead continued:

In certain country districts natives are forced to live under shockingly insanitary conditions, without amenities essential to human life. No proper lighting or heating facilities, cesspools all too often having to fulfil the need of even an outside lavatory. There are areas where the families on rich men's land, men, women and children, are forced to exist without the privacy a cow would have in its own shed. These flea-ridden hovels should be condemned. Instead of certain publicity hunting personalities seeking popularity by donating sums of money publicly to charitable causes – however deserving – concern should first be given to having their own homes in order. Wealthy men come down from the North and elsewhere to buy up lands for exploitation and their own benefit. This should be stopped immediately until this County Council has first inspected and been assured that human beings have protection for a decent way of life. In the forthcoming local elections it is to be hoped that the public conscience will not be influenced – or bribed by pretty speeches and false promises – to cast its vote in favour of some greedy Lord Tom Noddy, masquerading as a saintly beneficiary to mankind. In outlying districts beyond our lovely Burnwood, there are . . .

Emma stopped reading, and put the paper down, before facing her father-in-law. Her cheeks had paled, though his were fiery red.

'Well?' he demanded again, 'what about it? *He* knew, didn't he – that wise-cracking Welshman, so did you? – that I was putting up for a seat? *You* knew as well it would be a starting point for Westminster when the time came? Yet you allowed *this* to go through—' he was waving the paper again, shaking visibly. 'Clear as daylight it is – "from the North – some greedy Lord Tom Noddy". What the devil's your game?'

He broke off, for want of breath.

For a second or two Emma was frightened, afraid he'd have a fit. But gradually his colour ebbed to a more natural, mottled shade.

'I knew nothing about it,' she said, shocked, but managing to sound calm and firm. 'Why should I? I'm only concerned with my own column. And anyway—'

'Yes?'

'You can't be sure Evan wrote it, and your name isn't mentioned.'

'It doesn't *have* to be, does it?' Sarcasm had replaced the momentory abuse in his voice. 'It's libel just the same. The snobs will love it, mop it up and snigger over their whiskies in their select clubs — I could be a laughing stock. I've a good mind to take it up — fight a case. That would stir things up all right. Your Welshman would be done for; because take my word on it, I'd win, and break him.'

'You can't be sure.' Her quick mind took a fighting turn. 'Wouldn't it be safer, and far cleverer of you to *use* this — this article?'

He looked momentarily nonplussed.

'Use it? How?'

'By taking it up. Agreeing. Make yourself a real power to do good. Visit these — these hovels. Contact the people, especially round Coldale. Speak the truth of your findings to the press, and get yourself talked about that way.' There was a pause in which his astonishment turned to grudging acknowledgement of her perspicacity. Then she continued, 'Once you've made an impact you can surely be subtle enough to win the other side. After all — they *are* rather a smug lot, aren't they?'

'Smug? Maybe. But—'

'Really,' she interrupted, 'it's your chance — if you've the guts and will to tackle it. Taking a case against Evan wouldn't solve anything, not to your advantage. It would just give him an opportunity to flaunt his ego and personality.'

He studied her with slowly awakening respect. 'By God,' he thought, 'she's of my own kind, a real clever one.'

'You may be right at that,' he said at last.

'I'm sure I am.'

Subdued and still amazed that anyone so feminine and in some ways fragile-looking as this young woman Arthur had married could have such businesslike astuteness, Jonathan, after a few cursory remarks, left Emma to her own thoughts.

Lloyd's explosive attack had surprised her as much as it had angered Jonathan, and at first she had been dismayed. The conclusion, however, had been satisfactory, up to a point. She might even take up the matter herself, presumably on Jonathan's side. Then he couldn't fight her at meetings. One thing she must keep clear to herself, however, and this was Jonathan's fierce ambition to get to Westminster. He musn't defy the existing hierarchy of the aristocracy too openly.

Which meant Evan must be a little more subtle in the immediate future.

*

It was the first week in September before Emma and Lloyd met again, on a Saturday about a mile from Oaklands. He was cycling round a bend bordering Feyland Woods, casually dressed, wearing knickerbockers and a loose jacket, with a camera slung over his shoulder. As her car approached up a slope in the lane, he jumped from his machine, grinning; with a grinding of brakes she drew the motor to a halt, and holding her skirt up in one hand, extricated herself through the door. When she'd started off from Eastwood early that afternoon she'd worn a hat tied under the chin with a gauzy scarf, but once away from the district she'd taken it off — flung it on the seat leaving her hair free in the breeze. Its dark rich russet shades gleamed copper-bright in the afternoon sunlight. Her short-caped lilac coat, loose at the neck, blended with the artistry of an Impressionist's painting against the background of early autumnal foliage. Shadows danced across the thread of roadway, dappling tree trunks and richly coloured leaves. Through net-worked branches the glimmer of a reservoir flashed momentarily, then faded behind a belt of slowly moving misted cloud. The smell of air — of damp earth already redolent with the first fallen leaves sent a wave of nostalgia through her whole body — a sensation of emotional hunger that quickly mounted to heady excitement, as she hurried towards Lloyd. It seemed, for that brief time, that they were the only two human beings in the world. No sign, no sound of anyone else. Just themselves together.

'Well, well,' he said, grasping her hand, and pulling her towards him. 'Who would have thought it?'

'What?'

'*You!* That we should meet like this. Or did you plan it, you loose woman?' The tones were jocular, but his eyes were not, holding a wealth of wonder and desire.

She laughed falsely. 'Don't be silly.'

'Is that all you can say?'

She shook her head. 'I've not anything to say at all really, except that I'll get on with that article, you know, the one about the poor living conditions — next week — if you'll print it. I think—' She swallowed, striving to keep matters on a normal level, but speaking mechanically, quickly, and with the words tumbling out. 'I think—'

He drew her close suddenly, so the warmth of his body, and steamy smell of his jacket overcame her with such longing, she did not for a few precious moments resist.

'Don't think, darling,' he whispered, with his lips hot against her cheek and ear. 'Emma, my love — please, this isn't just chance — it's inevitable. We've both known it, from the beginning. Let me love you, Emma—'

With a terrible effort she pulled herself away.

'We mustn't. Not here. Not — not *ever*.' Before he knew her intention she'd turned and rushed back to the car. He caught her hand again before she got in, and twisted her round once more to face him.

'What's the matter with you? Frightened?'

She nodded. 'Perhaps — I don't know.'

'What of? — *Him?* Bradley?'

'Maybe. Or — there are other things.'

'The paper? Your reputation?'

'In a way. It has to be, hasn't it? My father would expect it.'

'For you to be unhappy? Embittered and thwarted?'

'Oh, Evan, no. Please try and understand.'

He dropped her hand suddenly.

'I can't; I'm sorry — life's too short. Understanding doesn't come into it.' His eyes had become steely, his jaw was a hard line, though a small muscle throbbed at one side.

She was suddenly frightened, bewildered by herself, her own feelings, his, and the issue which in so short a time had assumed terrifying reality. Lloyd would never be satisfied by dreams only; neither would she. They wanted everything, both of them. And so much was at stake. But if she lost him — the idea was unbearable. Desperately she fought for self-control, to be logical. It was impossible.

'Evan—'

'Yes?'

'Don't be like this. It's not fair. You know how I feel, but give me time; *please*—'

'What for? To think?'

'Yes. *Yes*.' Her voice and manner were sharp, fierce, 'I'm not just a — just a—'

'Farmer's wench all set for a roll in the hay? Right. If that's the way you see things, Mrs Bradley—'

'It's *not*. You know it's not!' She caught his sleeve impulsively, and when he forced himself to look down again into the clear grey of her shining limpid eyes, the anger and hot desire in him relaxed suddenly into something gentler and more compassionate. She wasn't playing with him. Just for a second or two he'd doubted her. But the sincerity of her gaze, the half-opened lips, and trembling form held no guile or sophistry. She was all longing, all woman — a virgin nymph lost in the labyrinth of wild instinct, and conventional conscience. As the muscles of his body eased and the hammering of his heart quietened, the truth of the situation registered with a certainty that annoyed him. Her virginity! he'd hit on it. It was true. No man had as yet bespoiled or claimed her pristine innocence. Not even that twisted swine Arthur she'd married. Then what *had* Bradley wanted of her?

'Emma—' He heard himself saying hesitantly.

'Yes?'

'I'm sorry for upsetting you.'

She shook her head. 'You haven't. Not really. I should have known. I'm as responsible as you. And I'm not a defenceless child. If you must know − I *wanted* you to go all wild and passionate and like you are − *exactly* like you are. I'm not a prig, and—' Gold flecks flew to her grey eyes challengingly. 'If you really love me − nothing else matters, not a damn!' Her stubborn little cleft chin and pert nose were set at a luminous angle. 'So if you like—'

Such longing rose in him his voice was husky, thick.

'Are you sure? Certain you won't regret—'

'Yes. Arthur doesn't count at all. If he'd been different − but he isn't; he's awful. Oh Evan − Evan—' Her arms reached to his neck. Shaking himself, he lifted her up, with his lips against her throat, carried her down a short path into the wood. After laying her down, he forced himself to leave her, remembering his bicycle and wheeled it swiftly through the undergrowth into the shadows of the trees.

When he returned to her, she was lying in the grass, with her hair unpinned, its copper lights rippling through crushed and springing bluebells; her eyes were wide, staring upwards through a tangle of silver birch and larch. Her pale elfin face was patterned by a tracery cast from quivering young leaves above. Her bodice was loose at the neck, showing the creamy whiteness of her slender neck. Yet there was nothing of the seductress about her − only a magical aura of undefiled passion and innocence awaiting fulfilment.

He knelt down, trembling, and took her hands, one by one, raising them to his lips; she smiled, and deliberately unbuttoned her gown, while desire mounted and hardened in him.

'Emma—' he whispered, '—oh God, it's so beautiful you are, *cariad*.' Unconsciously the lilting Welsh endearment blended with the hushed murmurs of the forest, of rustling undergrowth, distant faint trickle of a brook over stones, and her answering low-voiced 'Darling, darling,' until words were stilled between them, crushed into small cries and responses as his hands sought and ravished every secret curve and recess of her body. Beauty was everywhere. With limbs entwined, male and female were united not merely through physical need, but by the deepest ties and longings of humanity to be built of one entity, spirit and flesh.

For some time, when all was over, and they were at peace again, they lay side by side, watching the glimmer of sky fading behind the trees. He sat up presently, bent once more to kiss each breast, then took a lock of her hair and put it to his lips.

She stirred and reached for her bodice.

'It's getting late, isn't it?' she said. 'And I'm supposed to be at Oaklands.'

'And I'm supposed to be back at the office with photographs of some old ruin that's going to be restored. Now see what you've done — you witch!'

She laughed as he helped her to her feet.

'If anyone's seen my motor-car down the lane they may — think things,' she said, and then with genuine alarm, 'Oh Evan — suppose someone passed, and thought there'd been an accident or something — they'd recognise the car and go to the house. Do you think—?'

'No I don't,' he told her firmly. 'This lane's one of the loneliest in Burnwood, as you well know.'

'Yes, but some walker or a farm labourer—' A little frown creased her brow.

He drew her to him. 'My dear love, when *that* bridge comes we'll cross it. Anyway some day we've got to face the future, and I'm not one to cower in corners forever. Secret meetings may be necessary for a time, but only until we've found the guts to say "damn all" to society.'

She shivered faintly.

'What's the matter? Cold, love?'

'No. Just—'

'Frightened?'

'Of course not. Why should I be? Well, maybe I am — a bit. Not of us, or because of loving. For you, I think, mostly.'

'Me?'

She nodded. 'It may alter things for you rather badly, Evan, when they know. We *must* wait a bit; for both our sakes. Your career's important. Don't deny it!'

'Temporarily, maybe. Only that.' He paused, then continued, 'I won't deliver the bomb-shell yet. Just remember one thing though—'

'Yes?'

'We belong. And there's nothing in the world can change it.'

*

By a freak of chance, Emma met Arthur returning from the paddock as she drove the motor-car down a side drive to its allotted shed. She called it her garage; her husband referred to it contemptuously as 'a stye' in contrast to the smart building specifically erected for Jonathan's Rolls.

The delight in her heart ebbed to discomfited irritation. The last person in the world she wished to see just then was Arthur. But he waited until she'd parked 'the jalopy' — another of her husband's disparaging nicknames, and walked with her up the main side drive leading to Eastwood's front door.

'Oaklands again, I presume?' he said in an offhand manner.

'And other places,' she answered quickly. 'Why?'

He gave her an alert, sidelong look. 'You look radiant,' he answered. 'Different. What have you been up to, Emma?'

Unable to help the hot flush rising to her cheeks, she forced annoyance into her voice, hoping to divert his attention by a show of anger.

'Oh don't be ridiculous. Driving. Just *driving* — I do sometimes, you know, merely for the pleasure of it. Anything wrong in that?'

His handsome face darkened. 'Only *you* know. But there are times when it might be advisable for you to have a bit of a gallop with me. That new gelding the pater presented you with needs exercise, and we should be seen together sometimes, don't you think?'

'Aren't we? If ever we're invited out I join you. At the dances — that horrible aristocratic charity ball affair you managed to get involved in—'

'There's no reason to rub it in. I *got* there, that's the important point. The Bradley name registered.'

'And did you enjoy it? The dance? The toasting and back-slapping — the noise and fuss?'

'Of course. What the devil are you getting at?'

'*I* didn't,' she answered recklessly, 'enjoy it, if you must know. It was all so beastly snobbisly *obvious*. And you! — the way you flattered and fawned over Bettina Carnley — *Lady* Bettina,' she added meaningfully. 'Do you imagine people didn't notice?'

His underlip took a sullen thrust. 'She's a very attractive woman. And influential. If anyone noticed, all the better. I'm going along with my father for once, distributing my charms where they're appreciated by all concerned.'

'Oh I'm sure she must have been positively *thrilled* by your male attributes.' The sting in her words did not escape him. He gripped her arm hard, making her wince.

'You just wait, madam,' he said in a threatening undertone, close against her ear. 'I've taken a hell of a lot from you, but any more jibes and you'll need *two* bustles on your charming posterior for a week or more.'

'Don't be so vulgar,' she said, shaking herself free. 'I hate your — your threats and bullying, Arthur Bradley. Leave me alone, or I'll—'

'You'll do nothing but what you're told to,' he said. 'And now—' as they neared the terrace, '—pull yourself together. Remember your place, and who you are.' The hard glitter in his eyes melted slightly. 'It's a pity you can't accept things, Emma. You still intrigue me. Can't you try and make a go of our life? You've got everything you want except—'

'Normality,' she interrupted. 'Yes, I know.'

'Is normality so important? Anyway — is anyone completely normal? Are *you*? Always tripping off to newspaper gatherings and business meetings? And that Welsh fellow — Lloyd? Is *he*? To my mind he's an excessive phoney braggart with a dangerous tongue. *Now* I hear you're going to collaborate with him on some challenging social problem of housing; presumably with my father's blessing, in the belief it will give him a leg up in local government.' He paused. 'You must be crazy, both of you.'

'Thank you.' Her voice had become ice.

Before they went into the house he touched her hand tentatively.

'Emma—' he drew her to a halt. Her body went rigid. 'Tonight I'll try and show you I do care for you in my way. You never know — tonight perhaps—'

Recalling past experiences she shuddered inwardly, thinking 'Oh no, not that, dear God. Not that.'

'It's all right, Arthur,' she forced herself to say brightly. 'I believe you. And don't worry, I'll try to behave more as you wish me to. And certainly we'll go riding. You're quite right about the gelding. He needs exercise. I've been very remiss.'

He was mollified. 'That's all right. We could go for a canter tomorrow perhaps — call en route on that old fellow Lord Wendle. The pater's well in with him and hoping the friendship will pay off.'

She felt a brief stirring of pity for him. He was like his father, so naïve — so completely ignorant of the tightly-knit, inherent perspicacity and loyalty of society's élite, one to the other. Wendle of course was something of an eccentric and oddity to his kind. But beneath the genial facade was a patronising quick-wittedness which would have surprised Jonathan had he guessed the extent of it. They had each other's measure, up to a point; each one was using the other to mutual advantage. Beyond that, familiarity ceased. The class bridge remained, and would be erased only by the passing of generations.

Still, so long as her father-in-law achieved superficial acceptance and his eventual seat in Parliament, Emma supposed that Bradley wouldn't care about deeper values. Money could do so much, and would probably, even in the end manipulate an advantageous marriage socially for Jessie. But happiness?

Poor Jessie.

Even her mother feared for her future. Her blunt personality and earthy rustic looks were hardly likely to stir romance in any young man's heart — especially some aristocratic snob out only for her dowry and money. Although Amelia herself was comparatively content and could no longer envisage living the humble life of her origins, she sensed Jessie's lack of confidence and incapacity to live up to the standards Jonathan expected of her. She had been taught to be well-mannered and dress tastefully. But the fact was that no clothes, however expensive, looked right on her. She simply had no outward charm, and Amelia knew that finishing school could never change, or supply the lack. In a more simple society — on the wild moors of her ancestry, she would probably have settled down easily with some steady young fellow who'd appreciate sound qualities of honesty, strength and physical health — Jessie's only attributes necessary for the making of a good wife and mother.

More than once Amelia had heard her husband refer to their daughter as a throw-back. On one occasion her blood had boiled in a flood of resentment.

'And if she is, what of it?' Amelia had asked bluntly. 'It's healthy stock she comes from, Jonathan Bradley, and don't you forget it. One day that sturdy girl of ours may make thee proud. There's other things in the world than silks an' satins an'—'

'All the liquor you consume in secret,' Jonathan had interrupted sharply.

There'd been a sullen, quiet pause, then, 'There's no secret about it. I hide nothing, and I'm not ungrateful for what you've done for me, Jonathan. It's not myself I'm grumbling about. But Jessie's my own. I bore her. I don't want her hurt.'

'She won't be. I'll see her secure. As secure as Arthur, though he doesn't appear to need any help from me. A handsome young ram if ever there was one.'

With a flash of insight Amelia had retorted unconsciously resorting to her North County brogue, 'Mebbe it would have been better for him if he'd had less of it.'

'Of what?'

'*Charm*. Looks. They're not allus an advantage. There's other things; such as—' She paused, struggling for the right word.

'Yes? Well, go on; have your say.'

'I will an' all; just to give you something to think about, Jonathan Bradley. I've allus kept quiet about Arthur's failings, for your sake, and because I'm so proud of him — mostly. But there's a sly side to him that puzzles me — specially with that grand, haughty look on him. And he can be cold. Heartless. I don't like that. He's got no kindness in him unless it suits his purpose. And that's what I meant about "those other things" — warmth, respect for others — to be able to give sometimes with naught in return. I reckon we've both failed in teaching the lad proper values.'

As she stopped speaking the rich colour in her face had faded visibly. For a moment or two her husband was speechless. It was the first time he remembered, since their marriage, Amelia being so forthright or having the courage to criticise him. He'd stared at her with a rare unexpected respect.

'That's quite a speech for you. Amelia. *Values!* So you think we've failed, eh?'

She'd shaken her head slowly. 'Sometimes I don't know what to think, and that's the truth. You asked me some time back, to sound him about him and Emma. Their marriage. But it's no good. Any mention of her name and he shuts up like a clam. And she's the same. Mind you, *I* can get on with her, she's a nice enough girl beneath all that intellectual talk. But there's no real *contact* between us. Well, there couldn't be, could there? — me coming from where I did, and *her* a *Fairley*.'

'I wish you'd stop harping on your background,' Jonathan snapped. 'You're my wife. That should be enough. Apparently it isn't though—' His gaze and voice had become resentful, moody. 'You have to have your liquor too, as well as fine clothes and rich food.'

'Aye,' she'd admitted, as she had, countless times before, sounding sad, resigned. 'Bucks me up when I'm down. There's many others like me, I reckon, with nothing much else in their lives but money.'

'If you took a bit of exercise now and then you'd probably feel fitter and certainly look better.'

'A bit late now,' she'd said.

Following the revealing conversation Jonathan had tried to dismiss his wife's criticism of their son from his mind, diverting his attention almost fanatically to business affairs, wheedling or blundering his way — some would have said, buying — into any important Leyford organisation available — donating gifts throughout the county to charitable concerns, with the satisfaction, later, of seeing his name printed as a member of worthy and respected committees. The Bradley name became synonymous with wealth and power. Despite innuendos and sly comments behind newspapers and brandies in select clubs, it could not be denied that with his guts and wherewithal Jonathan was steadily becoming a force to be reckoned with.

The old adage was true.

Money counted.

Gradually members of the élite bearing handles to their names — deigned to visit social functions at Eastwood — including a garden party on behalf of a certain charity attended by forefront personalities including a wealthy Maharajah and a fox-hunting Duchess who, following her recent divorce, had her eye on an eccentric minor member of Royalty. On a more intellectual level, the gardens of Eastwood were thrown open for a week's performance of Shakespeare, the proceeds of which were to be donated to a Welfare Fund for the unemployed and disabled. In the autumn of 1904 a masked ball was given in which servants of the house and two neighbouring large establishments were invited to join. Jonathan, while ploughing his way up the social ladder, never lost sight of the fact that when election time came the man-in-the-street would have a powerful part to play. Therefore, a little ploy to go ahead would pay off.

Before these events, however, his newspaper the *Comet* had a set-back, originating, he was doggedly certain, through Emma's article on the housing question.

She wrote it with fire and zeal in pungent terms which she'd not entirely realised until then that she possessed. Her sensitivity indeed, had been shocked when she visited the area of the benighted dwelling. It stood on the outskirts of Coldale, and in two rooms with a shanty outhouse, housed three generations of human beings, men, women and children; it was damp, with a leaking roof, a cess-pit not far from the door, and flea ridden. The inmates were belligerent, with a hopeless air of fatigue about them. The son and father were unemployed miners — the former through a pit closing, the second through silicosis.

There was no political reference to any party in Emma's comments; her attack was on governing authorities whom she accused of turning a blind eye on the distressful circumstances in which a certain sector of the population was condemned to live.

The effect when printed under bold headlines on the front page of a Friday edition of the *Echo*, followed by an extended version in the weekly, was electric. Letters followed immediately, demanding action, and condemning landowners who came from other parts to increase their wealth through Leyford industry which had made it the richest town in England.

Jonathan was furious — especially as Emma had used her maiden name of Emma Fairley instead of Bradley for the write-up. He blamed his daughter-in-law irately for this.

'And what did you think you were doing?' he demanded, waving the sheet at her. 'Putting me back a bit? Old prejudices, eh? Destroying all I've achieved during these last months? And Fairley! Why the devil did you have to call yourself that?'

'I'm known by it. It was my name.'

'Was — *was*. Aye!' he thumped his chest. 'But that's all over, by God. You're a Bradley now, and the idea of this — this writing business was to pull it up a bit. Help *me*. Me — d'you understand? Oh yes, you do all right. You're a deep one. You must've calculated in your mind for quite some time how to get the *Echo* on your side and poke fun at the *Comet*.'

Emma's lips went tight. Her voice was cold when she said, 'I didn't calculate at all. I spoke the truth. What I saw *shocked* me. You didn't come into it at all.'

'And who put you up to it? Who told you about that slum

place at all? – It was him, wasn't it? – The Welsh fellow Lloyd?'

Evading a direct answer Emma said, 'Evan's the editor of the newspaper. I have to consult him about any story.'

'Oh! so it's Evan now, is it?' The question was a bitter sneer. 'Well, my girl, it won't be much longer. There are political aims behind this drivel I don't like at all. You may think you've got the upper hand on the *Echo* at the moment, but you're mistaken. Fifty-one per cent of the shares! Eh? Well – with forty-nine of them gone, or near enough, that rag of your father's will be defunct. Nil. Worth nothing but for the waste-paper basket. I'll break Lloyd, by God I will. This business may have broken any chance I had of getting on to the Council.'

Whether the article was partly responsible for Jonathan's forecast, which proved weeks later to be true, was doubtful. The fact was he failed, by a minority, to be elected. That the authorities moved quickly to have the unfortunate families decently housed weighed nothing at all with him. No human factor counted. The damage was done. And to him it was all Emma's fault. In public, however, he put on a brave front, an air of bonhomie and almost genial acceptance which deceived most, hence the parties and social occasions at Eastwood. At such a crucial point in his life he recognised the importance of being judged as nothing but an honest fair-minded man. The great challenge lay ahead when the country gave its vote. For that day all potential obstacles must be effectively squashed, and the priority was to see that Evan Lloyd was got out of the way for good.

Emma did her best to appease Jonathan's disappointment by keeping her column, following the argument, on a lower key, and even in assuming a friendlier facade to Arthur. In public they represented a devoted young couple, to the majority of people. Arthur, fiercely jealous if he thought she appeared too interested in any other man, took fanatical pride in showing her off as his wife and therefore his unique possession. In private, life to her, was hell. She no longer fought him as she had at the beginning of their marriage; once in the past when she'd defied him, he'd flung her on the bed and abused her by not only slapping her soundly, but in other ways that had made her want to die. He had never used the whip – yet. And she had determined he never should. Having to bear his warped endearments was odious to her, but her apparent acquiescence reduced these eventually to a minimum. In fact he was beginning to tire of trying to goad her, and boredom led him to drink.

Jonathan noticed, and was worried.

'For God's sake take a good look at yourself,' he said one day. 'Pull yourself together. What's the matter with you? You've got all you want, haven't you? Wealth, looks, a handsome wife – and the time's approaching when you can be a help to me – to us all, the whole family, if you put your mind to it. Wendle's got it all fixed for me as candidate in the election, and it won't be long, lad, after that – a knighthood maybe, hereditary. Think where that puts you—'

'Me?' Arthur sneered derisively.

'Yes, you. My *son*.' There was a pause during which Jonathan's mind took another direction. 'Emma,' he said, 'your wife. She's not – cold is she, frigid? If that's it there *are* other women. Don't think I'd blame you—'

Arthur flung back his handsome head, gave a laugh as harsh and cold, despite the liquor he'd consumed, as the ice-flame of his eyes. 'Women! when the day comes I depend on any one of them I may as well be dead.'

He turned abruptly and marched, tall, arrogant, Nature's perfection in physical form, down the drive to the stables, where his stallion waited, eager for a gallop.

Such rides generally ended at a remote cottage on the edge of a lonely copse. The humble dwelling was inhabited by a farm labourer's widow and her twelve-year-old son, David. The woman, Cora, eked out a living by making brooms, and during the summer months selling daffodils and bunches of posies in Leyford. The boy, not too bright in the head, occasionally accompanied her. He was black-haired, unusually good-looking, and accepted gleefully the present taken to him by Arthur. In the privacy of the woods favours were equally bestowed. Their understanding was mutual, a secret carefully guarded, even from Cora, who conveniently left them alone together when necessary. She asked no questions; silence on the situation was golden in every sense.

Had Jonathan remotely suspected the depths of his son's depravity he'd doubtless 'have kicked him out' in his own terminology.

But he hadn't.

10

By the end of September Lloyd found himself in the unhappy position of editing a newspaper that was certainly on the downgrade financially. This was not due to any withdrawal of local support, but by pressure put on its production by Bradley. Although a completely united board could ensure continuance – through Emma's support – of its policy, she had neither the means nor devious knowledge required to thwart Bradley's aim. His mind so fanatically set in getting rid of Evan, conceived a number of subtle ways of achieving it. Firstly, he managed to get the two largest shareholders next to Emma and himself on to his side, then began manipulating advertisers against the *Echo*'s increasing 'new look'. Much of the revenue from sales depended on two pages devoted almost entirely to advertising – sometimes a full sheet was used by one business firm. Without income from this quarter the paper would indeed have a struggle to survive. Closure eventually would be inevitable. Jonathan's methods were brilliantly cunning; the cost to his own pocket was considerable – at the beginning. On the other hand, reimbursement soon followed by once more achieving rising circulation of the *Comet*.

Evan gradually found his hands tied from several angles. His chief reporter was lured to join the staff of the new paper, with a

high rise in salary, and the promise of further advancement
money-wise and in status when the *Echo* was eventually amalgamated into the proposed *Midlander*. New machinery was
needed for printing and better transport for distribution.
Emma, seeing how things were going, was desperate, no longer
so much on her late father's behalf — he was dead and could no
more be here — but for Lloyd, whom she so passionately loved
and admired. During recent weeks they had managed to meet
secretly, and as time passed had realised an inevitable crisis
must soon be faced.

'It can't go on like this,' he told Emma, when they met one
late afternoon in his office for discussion, presumably, of her
column. 'Neither can the paper. I'll have to quit, and that's the
truth of it.'

Dismay filled her as though a dark cloud had descended,
sucking her into a dark well of misery. Until that moment she'd
not accepted the possibility of life without Lloyd. Their
moments of real intimacy, physical and mental, it was true,
were few. But his image — the memory of his sudden, elfin
smile, the clear eyes that could be so bright and piercing one
moment, the next warm with desire and longing filled her days.
His touch, the feel of his arms round her, of his body, close
against hers, made her a new person, revitalised her will so that
she could endure — without displaying how hateful it was — her
life at Eastwood with Arthur. Pain gnawed her as she asked,
'Leave the *Echo*, you mean? But what will you do? Perhaps the
Courier—'

Evan shook his head.

'No thank you, darling. If I quit the *Echo* I quit the problems
of financial journalism. Freedom! I've got to have it, Emma.
Bradley means to get his hand on the whole group of Midland
newspapers, and in my opinion he may do it. The *Courier* will
fight, and it may, it just *may* endure. But the tycoon warfare
sickens me. Money — grab all — possessions? What does it all
amount to? You tell me.'

'It can advertise you. Make your name known as a poet,' she
said stubbornly. 'Don't you want *that*? You've got such a gift—'

She broke off as he walked to a window overlooking the street. Outside it was a perfect early autumn evening. The last rays of gold sunlight dappled streets and the few trees, touching the forms of passing pedestrians and colourful glory of leaves and herbage. A faint drift of woodsmoke crept into the room through the open window. All was still; a few lights glimmered from a factory on the opposite side of the canal, giving the impression of square eyes watching. A moment in time that could have been magical to both of them − *was* magical but filled for Emma with aching, nostalgic despair.

'Of course I want recognition,' she heard him say. 'Not because I'm dubbing myself a genius or pioneer, but because of *this*—' He turned suddenly, thumping his chest. 'Something *inside* me I want to say − something that's *real* and important and will perhaps give impetus to others. It may sound phoney − the kind of cant loafers use when they damn well shy away from a day's decent hard work. But I'm not that kind. I'm *hungry*, Emma. Hungry to express myself, to get to the heart of things in the way I choose − travel perhaps, adventure − share with them all, young and old, sick, healthy, black or white, discover what I was born for—' He broke off, smiled in the whimsical way that so touched her, and confessed '—Well, maybe I've done that already.'

He crossed the floor quickly, and took her in his arms. She closed her eyes, feeling suddenly so glowing and comforted, nothing else for a few seconds registered. Then she remembered.

'You're trying to say − telling me − you're going away?' she asked.

'I don't know. If I do it won't be for ever. It will be because I have to plan for us both, *cariad*.' The old endearment slipped out instinctively.

'But *where*? Wales?'

He drew her to the window. They both stood there, watching the first frail cloud of mist shimmer the water, taking figures and slowly moving traffic into blurred silhouette.

'Perhaps,' he answered after a pause. 'I'm known there, and

it's my home. I have my degree — I'm qualified — there are
many clubs — where lecturers are needed. I've connections that
would earn a week's keep by travelling about. It might even be
possible to come to Leyford officially from time to time. The
university and working men's college are both getting quite go-
ahead. We wouldn't be *parted*, darling.'

'Wouldn't we?' Her voice was full and filled with doubt. 'How
often would we see each other?'

'As often as I could damn well make it. You know that.'

'How do I know?'

The arm round her waist tightened. With eyes blazing down
into hers, his lips came full and firm on her mouth, driving for
that sad-sweet interval all emotion and passion from her.

She loved him; oh God — so much, so much. Not only his
potent sexuality, his vitality and fire, but his brilliant quick
mind, combined with a certain ruthless honesty that would
inevitably lead him into dangerous confrontation with any
placid status quo of society. His poetry too. Beneath the man of
action was ever the dreamer, the romantic Celt in whose genes
flowed still the fanatical love of his own land, who could bring
lost legendry to life again in words, and make music of common
everyday things: the miner eking out his days and energy underground in the pit; a hard working farmer's wife, baking bread in
her small kitchen; the tramp of pedestrians' feet plodding to
their homes down grey Welsh streets through the rain; and,
beyond, the mountains, grim and bleak with their peaks inky
black against a winter sky. The swirl of rivers coursing through
narrow dark valleys past hamlets and towns towards the coast;
and singing — forever the singing, not only of men's voices from
taverns and clubs, but of an emotional longing and hunger bred
in the very blood and genes of the Welsh: the inheritors.

Therein lay Evan's background and his gift. Through his
senses he conveyed the unique richness of his ancestry, which
was a curious blend of the worker and the scholar. His father
had been a humble but dedicated mining engineer, his mother
the fiery beautiful daughter of a well-educated schoolmaster of
stern religious views. Their marriage had been against the

wishes of both families, and had proved, later, to be a stormy one. But it had survived. Iestyn Lloyd had died in a mining accident when Evan, his son, was eleven years old, and Angharrad, his daughter, seven. Marged, the widow, refusing help from her parents had taken a post as village schoolmistress at a remote hamlet in the valleys, bringing up her children with a strictness against which Evan had rebelled. Fiercely, independently, he had worked his way through College, obtaining a literary degree. It was during that period his mother had been killed, also his sister, when a mountainous tip of coal refuse slid one tragic wet day, claiming many victims.

Evan had regretted her death, but not mourned her from the heart. She had been too stern, too violent. But the loss of little Angharrad and his father had sewn seeds of defiant pain in him which remained with him, at the root of his being, and always would.

He never spoke of such things, not even to Emma. But in his verse the dormant anguish surfaced occasionally with a poignancy that was almost discomforting. Emma was curious. If only he would open up to her, she'd thought more than once. It seemed to her they should share everything. Nothing should be withheld from two people in love as they were. She'd probed, and all he'd said was, 'Let the dead rest. Yours and mine. It's the future we have to plan for. That's what I mean to do.'

This was true, of course, and when she'd reviewed the situation objectively, she'd realised that she, also over certain matters, was as secretive as he was, in withholding the painful intimacies of her life with Arthur. So they were quits, in a way — but with a difference. Lloyd, now, was twenty-eight, and had admitted, without giving any specific details, that he'd had more than one love affair, omitting to reveal a certain interim that might, at that time, have changed Emma's whole attitude to him. As it was, one painful question gnawed her. Supposing, if he returned to Wales for an interim, there was some girl or woman waiting for him, to whom he once again was drawn and fell for?

What would she do?

How could she bear it?

It mustn't happen. It *mustn't*.

Suddenly, on that aching, nostalgic Autumn afternoon, she pulled away from him, and said.

'No, you can't. You *can't*.' Her small chin was set, her grey eyes tortured.

Dismay filled him. He was hurt — for both of them, but at that moment mostly for her. He was experienced and could be hard when necessary, but her innocence made her specially vulnerable. During past weeks he'd toyed with the idea of their taking off together immediately. But male practicality told him that in doing so they would both be so chained by circumstances the foundation of their union might suffer and wither into a grey dutiful struggle to exist. This mustn't happen, for her sake more than his.

'I've told you — I may *have* to,' he said gently. 'I shall be seeing you — never doubt that — oh, my darling, you must have faith. Once I've the wherewithal — a responsible post, or proper means of supporting you, I shall be down to carry you off with me on some fine steed, like knights in the *Mabinogian*.'

'The *Mabinogian*?'

'A Welsh book of legends,' he told her — 'a very ancient one. Traditional.'

His effort at humour brought a slight travesty of a smile to her lips.

'And suppose—' She broke off hesitantly.

'Suppose what?'

'If Arthur—'

'If the swine maltreats you,' he asserted, 'I've told you — that's different. I'll come immediately from wherever I am, and kill him.'

The touch of melodrama restored a vein of common sense in her.

'I wouldn't want that. And you wouldn't do it anyway. You're no potential murderer. And — you needn't worry — Arthur's never harmed me — physically.' The half-lie stuck in her throat, but her statement, combined with a return of rose colour to her cheeks, deceived him. He breathed a sigh of relief.

'Is there anything else?' he asked. 'Anything I can do, to make things easier? Be honest now. You understand?'

She nodded.

'I'm trying.' Then forcing a light tone into her voice, 'Just so long as you haven't another girl tucked away somewhere I'll survive, I suppose. Is there?'

His look was whimsical — full of mischief when he answered, 'Plenty. Black-haired, blondes, and redheads.' The banter died. 'Oh Emma,' he said, 'you shouldn't ask such a thing — even in fun.'

'No. I suppose not.'

'One day,' he continued, looking away from her at some paper on his desk, 'when everything's sorted out, I'll reveal the extent of my murky past, if you insist. It's not important anyway. The present, and the future's our problem.'

'Yes, yes, I know.' With an effort she dispelled a sense of hopelessness rising in her. 'And if you're really determined to go, that's it. I can understand, see your point. The paper isn't all *that* important.' Her voice trembled slightly.

'It's very important,' he asserted, 'or *was*. To you, especially. But against Jonathan Bradley, Emma, its chances of survival now are nil. And I don't intend being kicked out. I'm going.'

'When?' Her voice was firm, hard, but her throat ached.

'As soon as possible. We may see each other again first — or not. I don't know. But we shall be in contact, and one day there'll be no more goodbyes between us. You must trust me.'

'Evan—' She stepped towards him again, her grey eyes bright. 'Evan—'

'No tears,' he said. 'I couldn't stand it. And you're not the crying sort.'

'No.'

She picked up her scarf and went to the door.

'All right, it's goodbye then — or au revoir—'

'I'll write. To Oaklands.'

'Yes.'

Little more was said, and a moment or two later Emma was in the street walking mechanically towards her car. Twilight was already a veil of fading blue-green over the town, evoking an eerie sense of melancholy and bygone long-dead things; roofs and chimney-pots loomed blurred and grey through a rising mist. Thin chords of sadness tugged at her chest, like the taut strings of some ancient violin about to break on an old nostalgic tune. Nothing seemed real. The pale squares of factory windows glared with the haunting quality of empty eyes over pavements and the canal. As she neared the car an old man shuffled by, head bent, as though unseeing, to the ground. A woman stood at the corner waiting — for what? Her lips even in the deepening light were brilliantly red. Her eyes slanting and pointed like those of a creature in a dream. So many lives! So many ways, differing destinies bred of human demands, despairs, and ambitions. Fulfilment and frustration; the pattern of existence.

Shivering slightly, Emma tore herself from such uncharacteristic melancholy, cranked up the car, and was presently on her way from the town to the more wooded area of Burnwood.

The country was beautiful, even in the half light. A number of russet and amber leaves still clung to the tracery of dark branched trees. Once, near the old ruin of the ancient Priory, she drew to a halt and sniffed the damp air and woodsmoke deep into her lungs. Old emotions were reborn, old memories from her childhood when the ancient spirit of 'place' had impelled her to write fairy-tales, and act them within the ivied walls. She smiled gently, though she didn't realise it. A certain bitterness in her was healed — temporarily. Always, she told herself, there was the forest, and Oaklands. The sanctuary that held something and always would, of her most secret self.

Presently she drove on again, not calling at her old home because it was too late.

When next she went that way, a week later, Evan Lloyd had left the *Echo* and it was to be a considerable time before she saw him again.

*

Once Evan had gone, Jonathan's attitude to Emma became more conciliatory – even a trifle benevolent.

'Don't think I'm going to try and wipe your family newspaper out,' he said, after delivering the news that Clarke was taking over until a new editor for the *Echo* was found. 'That's what you've been told, I suppose, by Lloyd and others like him. At the moment they're quite wrong. Eventually – it's possible; but we've a long way to go to get *The Midlander* established, and during that time there'll be plenty of opportunity to test the *Echo*'s value – financially, and to the public. In fact, there's no reason on earth why a revised weekly shouldn't continue indefinitely. Natives and country people look forward to hearing tasty bits and pieces, and any sensational event in their area—'

'Such as Births and Deaths,' Emma interrupted tartly. 'Round Burnwood especially the people are a closely knit group. It isn't only the extraordinary that appeals to them. They appreciate sound facts.'

'Exactly,' drily. 'Thanks for pointing it out.' The vein of sarcasm didn't make any impact on Emma's point of view regarding the Bradleys or the *Echo*. She had to accept that the end of an era had come with Lloyd's departure. Although he'd been editor for so comparatively short a time, he'd made his mark which had been resented by Jonathan. Whoever next filled the post would be less colourful and more of a 'yes man'. Yes to the Bradleys. Her father even might have given in – she didn't know. She wasn't certain at that point of anything very much at all. Her sense of drive, with Evan's departure, had temporarily died in her. While Lloyd was in the vicinity the knowledge had given excitement and hope to her life. Now, though she still hoped, all manner of doubts and possibilities clouded her spirits.

Jonathan was puzzled. He'd expected opposition and arguments from her, but not the bitterness, almost dull disinterest that gave him no challenge or pride in his achievement. He'd won. But victory was in a curious way tasteless – flat.

To Arthur Emma was more acquiescent. For the first time she felt mildly sorry for him, recognising that in spite of his extraordinary good looks and capacity to charm when he wished, he was actually no more than a tool under his father's thumb and had been since his birth, a product fashioned to further Bradley ambitions, a course that had driven him to his own furtive other life, and to alcohol. Beneath the air of arrogant sangfroid there lurked a childish sense of impotence and failure.

Once she had discovered the crumbling foundation beneath the ice-cold veneer, Emma found that dealing with Arthur's twisted personality became easier. She used subtle means of flattery when dangerous signs of temper showed, and in this way a sense of balance was restored.

'It isn't so bad for you after all, is it, Emma?' he enquired one night as she prepared for bed. She was wearing a silk wrap of a becoming peach shade that enhanced her glowing skin and the gleaming of her rich hair.

'What?' she asked, drawing a brush through the copper mane. Although she had a maid, she'd insisted from the first in dealing with her own toilette at nights.

'Us. You and I. Our marriage.'

'If you're contented, that's all that matters,' she answered, ambiguously.

'*You* matter,' he asserted, touching her neck with a caressing finger. He had slim hands, elegant and tapering, unlike either of his parents. The finger stroked the base of her skull, travelling downwards lightly over each delicate vertebra of her spine. The brush fell from her hand. Automatically she stiffened.

He noticed, laughed a little self-consciously, and said, 'Don't worry, I'm not up to anything, as you've put it more than once. I was merely pointing out that I still − care for and admire you. You're very beautiful.'

'Thank you.'

'And lately you've been so much more cooperative.' Through the mirror she saw his face peering questioningly at her reflection, waiting for a reply. 'I wonder *why*?' he added ruminatively in a way that discomfited her.

'Must there be a reason?' she forced a smile. 'I suppose I know you better, and have learned not to expect certain things most women do. Ordinary women.'

'Ah.' With both hands, he pulled the hair from her face and rolled it in a tight knot at the back of her head. 'There!' he continued, when the fine bones were quite clear and freed of any silken curl or shadowed tendril on her forehead. 'You could be a boy now − or a golden statue of some young Greek god. Greek gods were never ordinary, neither are you. You could be − magnificent, Emma.'

His tone was so abnormally rapturous, his bright blue eyes so filled with cold fire, she made a quick movement, jerked his hands away, and stood up, sending the dressing table stool to the floor, facing him. Inadvertently, the wrap fell away from one breast revealing its subtle sensuous curve and rosy nipple beneath the fragile nightdress. Hurriedly she pulled the wrap close to her neck as her hair fell loose again over her shoulders.

He stepped back, stood quite still for a moment regarding her with shocked disgust. Then he said contemptuously, 'Go to bed, cover yourself. You *disgust* me.'

'But—'

The cold lines of his lips turned into an ugly sneer.

'You heard what I said.'

'Yes, I heard, and I'm not staying. You get to your bed. *You* with your dreams of Greek gods and eunuchs. You're not sane, Arthur. And you know it. But does *he*? Your father?'

The question hit him. He wiped his brow with a shred of cambric, and sat on the bed, with his head in his hands. When he looked up, the glittering eyes had quietened to blue pools softened by unshed tears.

He pulled himself together with astonishing speed, assuming even a shred of dignity.

'Please stay,' he said, 'I'm sorry, *I'll* sleep in the dressing room. But—' the lips tightened again, 'I rely on you to say nothing of this to my father; you understand? − Anyway, he wouldn't believe you.'

'No.'

Feeling unutterably weary, she went towards the bed, and

stood there with her back to him, waiting for him to go. Only when she heard the dressing room door open and close, did she make a move. Then she flung herself on the quilt and lay there for some time staring unseeingly at the ornate encrusted ceiling.

'Evan,' she thought helplessly. 'Oh Evan — why did you have to go away?'

She knew the answer, Lloyd's answer, but somehow it made no sense. He should have been near at hand to comfort and prove his reality by fulfilment of their love. She didn't yet know that fulfilment had already been achieved, giving life to the flowering tiny seed in her womb; the fruit of their love — hers and Evan's.

11

Emma, on edge, restlessly waited for news from Evan for over a week, making an excuse each day for either riding by horse or car to Oaklands, on the pretext, when necessary, that she had business to attend to concerning renovations at the Dower House which meant visits to Leyford, and sometimes a certain furnishers in Charbrook dealing with fabrics in new Liberty designs. She had legitimate reasons also for concerning herself with the *Echo* column following editorial changes. There was at that time therefore no reason for suspecting her motives and absences at Eastwood. Jonathan congratulated himself that the purpose of getting rid of Lloyd had been so effectively achieved with the minimum of trouble. Emma appeared during those first days comparatively docile and ready to accept his interim plan for the newspaper. The truth was that she was so dulled with disappointment by Evan's apparent neglect that for a brief time she didn't care about much else. When, after ten days, there was no word — no note from him waiting at Oaklands, she managed to pull herself together and turned once more to business matters, becoming efficiently involved in the *Echo*'s future. It was obvious to her that there would now be no chance of revitalising it into anything but a rather dull, middle-of-the-road local news-sheet — a publication that would just manage to pay its way until the time came for its extinction through amalgamation into the future *Midlander*. There would be no controversy in its columns during its waning life, no fire or spark of individuality. Therefore — the sooner it went the better. But not the weekly. Her quick mind, searching for creative interest to fill the aching loss of contact with Evan, found, at last, a solution. Having so pleased Jonathan with her apparent acceptance of his recent policies, she had no difficulty in interesting him by her new and sudden brainwave.

'The weekly,' she said boldly one day, 'why shouldn't the weekly stand on its own feet? You say the *Echo* would cost a fortune in the new machinery required for its successful survival. Well then! You've not much faith in it, anyway, for the future, so let it go. But the weekly could continue on what equipment's already there. And extra sheets − a kind of supplement could be published with it, dealing exclusively with *women's* affairs. Do you understand?'

Jonathan regarded his daughter-in-law with bewilderment, but faint interest stirring.

'Go on,' he said, 'be more explicit. What do you mean? − *women's affairs?*'

'Yes, *yes*. Don't you see? Women are in need of some paper, some personal news-sheet or magazine of their own. They're quite uncatered for at the moment, especially in country districts. But tips on fashion, cookery, crafts, gossip of social affairs, perhaps a 'woman of the week' paragraph plus a photograph − competitions, even a question-and-answer on home affairs, and dressmaking − gardening—' She paused, watching interest quicken in his eyes, as potential possibilities of her idea took shape. 'Don't you *see?* It would pay off. Double the circulation of the weekly, and gather a whole lot of new readers. It could be a money-spinner, Jonathan.'

There was a pause, while his fingers drummed a sharp tattoo on the table. Then he said, 'You have an idea there, Emma, a constructive one, but whether it's practical or not's another question. Who'd run it, to begin with?'

'*I* could, within reason. I—'

'But you've the Dower House and family affairs to deal with, as well as your interest in Oaklands.'

She set her chin stubbornly. 'I'd have to have help, of course − but only a minimum of personal staff, two at the most, and—'

'And what would you propose to call it?' he asked. 'This new venture?'

'Oh, yes. The name would be important. We'd have to

think—' he appreciated the 'we' '—perhaps something like *Woman's View*, or – or *Women at Home* – no, not that, too suburban. *Woman's Post*, perhaps, *that* would bring in letters. I just don't know yet. We'd hit on the right thing in the end. Honestly, the whole thing *is* practical.'

The short discussion ended by Bradley saying he'd give her idea consideration, and with that she had to be satisfied.

Privately he'd half accepted the idea, marvelling at the girl's perspicacity. A woman's paper. Why not? Especially starting with Emma at the helm. There was no knowing – with proper handling and advertisement it might expand in public appeal and circulation far further than the boundaries of Leyfordshire.

The more he viewed the suggestion the more enticing it became, although he kept any growing enthusiasm he had to himself. When he mentioned the matter to Arthur, his son appeared at first superciliously amused, then faintly resentful. 'Don't say dear Emma has got under your skin that much,' he remarked. 'A *woman's* paper. You must be crazy.'

'Watch your tongue,' Jonathan snapped, 'and put that glass down.' Arthur was half leaning against the table with a whisky in one hand, and the decanter in front of him. His cold eyes flamed angrily; he was about to defy the command when Jonathan's expression made him think again. He obeyed, with a short laugh. 'Now,' Bradley continued, 'pull yourself together and try to take an intelligent interest in something other than horses and drink for a change. I don't know what's happened to you lately, or why. If you're unable to sire a son by that wife of yours, at least you can give a thought to business expansion and consideration of my own ambitions, which should also be yours. If there's any problem I can help with—'

Concern momentarily quietened his manner, and his voice.

'Problem?' Arthur echoed brightly. 'What could there be?' He jerked himself to apparent attention. 'As far as I can see everything's going fine. The *Comet*'s on its way up again, you've effectively squashed The *Charbrook Echo*. You seem to be heading for a pretty safe seat in Parliament when the time comes. But a woman's paper – well, if you're attracted by such an off-beat proposal, go ahead with it, and good luck to you. No doubt it'll please Emma. I shan't try to do anything to oppose it.'

'If you'd try a little harder in the way I want and beget a son,' Jonathan said acerbically, 'it would please me much more.'

'Such things happen, or they don't,' Arthur pointed out curtly. 'Perhaps Emma's barren. Anyway—' he smiled brightly, 'there's always Jessie. Why don't you cut short the finishing school affair and find some poor aristocratic mug in need of cash. My sister may not be a beauty, but I'd gamble a bit on her breeding ability.'

Jonathan turned away, faintly disgusted. But before ending the unsatisfactory interview he said coldly, 'Watch your step; I expect more than sarcastic comments and doubtful habits from my heir. You may be my son, but you can't hold a candle to your sister in character. And remember—' he rounded on his heel savagely to regard Arthur from hot angry eyes under beetling brows '—if I want to I can strike you out of my will, leaving you not a penny.'

'I see. Threats.'

'No, no. Not yet,' Bradley answered heavily. 'Just try and show more interest in family affairs and interests, and less in – in that stuff. The bottle.'

Emma meanwhile, flung herself feverishly into the idea, driven mostly by the necessity somehow of shutting Evan Lloyd out of her mind.

It wasn't easy; every time she took certain lanes through the forest the beauty and magic of rare moments she'd spent with him was revived achingly on a tide of memory threatening to pierce her armour. So she steeled herself to a harsh attitude of condemnation, almost contempt, of past weakness, when she'd imagined even for a brief second he could be in love with her.

Had he cared at all, she told himself, he'd never have left so suddenly. He'd have stayed at least in the district for a while so they could plan in some way for the future. There was the workingmen's college in Leyford where he'd suggested he might find employment as lecturer for a period – and the *Courier* – whatever he'd said about prospects there, he hadn't seemed interested in finding out. No. Facts had to be faced. For a time their romantic interludes had given him pleasure, but the bitter truth was that their relationship had not been sufficiently important to him for full committal. At first she'd made excuses for his silence — there could have been an accident — he was ill — or his letters had gone astray. Each time she called at Oaklands she asked the housekeeper, was there any post? Once, Rosalind's governess produced a bill, another time an envelope containing advertisements. But nothing, ever, from Evan.

On the last occasion of her enquiries the housekeeper regarding her more intently than usual, asked meaningfully, 'Are you expecting something very important, then?'

Realising that agitation and concern must have shown on her face, Emma had replied with more force than was necessary, 'Certainly not. I was hoping to hear from a friend that's all. Someone I knew a long time ago.'

She'd shrugged her shoulders, and without another word left the woman staring after her, and went to look for Rosalind.

She never asked again.

In the following few weeks her outward business-like dedication to plans for the weekly supplement combined with her authoritative views on the redecoration of the Dower House, deceived everyone but Arthur, who sensed beneath her cold mature manner something of the wounded sensitive girl beneath. Her new role certainly made her, from his point of view, easier to get on with. She expected no emotional response from him any more, no gentleness, and little courtesy except in company when he still played the gallant surprisingly well. So long as he could still show her off as a prize possession in public, he was satisfied. But his cynical quick mind had told him for some time that her new attitude was due to something else, beyond his orbit. Since Lloyd's departure she'd changed, and he resented any male influences in her life beyond his own. In his sane moments he knew he couldn't blame her if she'd taken a lover. Faithlessness wouldn't have mattered if he'd condoned it first. But if she'd played any game with him behind his back, then he'd have revenge — *somehow*. Jonathan knew nothing of these dark suspicions that occasionally set Arthur's temper on edge.

By January of 1905 it became clear that the Conservative Government might be facing a crisis in the year ahead. Following the Boer War, despite sturdy support in certain quarters for the aristocracy, the party was slowly being forced into a defensive position. The possibility of a new election before its time created restlessness in the minds of those who were at all interested in political matters. Jonathan was one of them. He intensified what before had been a more or less sleeping campaign, into active public demonstration cunningly contrived to win support from both sectors of the community.

The *Echo*, as Lloyd had foreseen, very gradually displayed a subtle Tory policy, which was subtly offset by Emma's weekly, *Woman's Post* which had been launched at an amazing speed, creating an instant readership. A go-ahead girl journalist eager for country life out of London, had been bribed by Jonathan at a high salary, to help, under Emma's editorship, also a secretary. Emma's energy was fanatical. The local newspaper world was agog with shocks and surprises; Jonathan was elated; having won Lord Wendle's support and being named as local candidate for the party, it seemed to him that everything was going his way. When the time came there'd be a fight. But he'd win. And already, in Emma, he was finding the satisfaction he'd hoped for, through his son.

Arthur, amused, cynical, mildly contemptuous of his father's ambitions for fame, allowed his charm and spectacular front to be utilised on Jonathan's behalf at the right times and in right places. Otherwise he continued with his own indulgences, increasingly aware, which others were not, except Amelia, that there was something curiously changed about Emma.

Emma for some time had suspected her own condition, but had refused to face the truth, telling herself stoutly women frequently missed periods for no apparent reason at all, except perhaps, emotional conflict or upset of some kind, and God alone knew she'd had plenty of both.

A day came in February, however, when she was forced to

accept reality. The weather was mild, for the time of year, lush
with the sense of pulsing new growth beneath the surface of
brown earth. After a tiring afternoon at the *Echo* offices, she
drove the car — still her father's old Mercedes — leisurely down
the threadwork of lanes leading to Oaklands. Through the
network of forest trees already feathered pale green with young
buds, the sky was pale grey-blue predictive of rising mist.
Beyond a clearing, as she passed, the tip of Hawkshill was
visible, crowned by a thin belt of cloud. How often, when a
child, she had climbed that particular hill, picking bluebells
and pretending she was a character from the ancient past —
some young princess who'd once had her castle where now only
a few stones and rocks remained.

The natural rocky tip of the hill was itself castle-like in
formation. 'Once a *great* mountain,' her father had told her,
'volcanic until the ice-age had covered it, and now millions of
years later only nine hundred feet of it are left.'

The atmosphere though, could not have changed all that
much, except that rabbits now hopped where once the great
dinosaurs had roamed. That particular afternoon, the sense of
elemental awareness in her seemed intensified. There was no
wind; the chug of the car's engine was the only sound to break
the utter stillness of the passing day; it was almost as though
time died, imprinting the muted picture of trees against dusky
blues and greens of fields, hedgerows and glint of water on her
mind forever. Always she had felt a deep inexpressible familiarity with the scene, but on this occasion there was a subtle
difference. Her heart, senses and whole being felt it. As she
neared Oaklands, a wild deer and fawn emerged from a copse
and stood watching while she drove by. Usually the animals, of
which there were plenty in the district, ambled away peacefully
at the approach of a human being or transport of any kind, but
this time it was as though a strange kind of recognition was
forged between them. Her stomach lurched then. A fleeting
wave of dizziness overcame her, taking everything into blurred
uncertainty. The experience was only momentary, but when it
passed, she knew.

She stopped the car and sat for several minutes thinking back. The deer and its young turned and disappeared again into the copse. A farm labourer crossed the lane a hundred yards or so ahead, driving cattle down a track towards fields bordering the woods. Bit by bit memories made sense — small insignificant things at the time which she'd ignored as mere 'nothings', a touch of indigestion, over-tiredness, eating the wrong food, a feeling of faint nausea that she'd put down to her increasing resentment and disgust at Arthur's touch or one of his snide remarks. And giddiness! — yes, there'd been that too, at intervals following an over-enthusiastic day dealing with the first editions of the *Woman's Post*. Why hadn't she thought of the answer before? Put two and two together and reached the logical answer so that she could have planned along slightly different lines? The paper, of course, and agitation concerning Evan. If she hadn't been so desperately anxious, ill-at-ease, and over-enthusiastic concerning the weekly she'd have known earlier that she was with child.

The shock registered then, in a wave of sudden lonely longing. Evan's child, and he wasn't there — was nowhere around to contact or confide in. Oh God! what a mess. How beautiful, rich and rewarding everything could have been — however difficult, if he'd been at hand to share and steer her through this awesome period of her life.

But he wasn't. Some day they might meet again, by chance; such a possibility though, would then be too late. She would have faced the inevitable in her own way, and he would have no part in it.

Nostalgia passed quickly into renewed resentment; she restarted the car with a jerk, driving the vehicle at its full speed, in a direct line for Oaklands. At the gate bordering the path leading round the rocky side of the house she didn't brake quite soon enough, and banged the frame and front mudguard clumsily. She sat a moment, shocked, feeling sickness rising in her. It quickly passed. She pulled the car door with a sudden rattle to get out, and after a brief inspection of damage done, made her way to the entrance.

Mrs Cox was hurrying down the hall when Emma went in.

'My dear,' she exclaimed, 'whatever was it? A crash?'

Emma waved a hand in negation. 'No, no. Just a slight mis-judgement. Nothing. I didn't brake properly. The gate will have to be repaired, but I'll see it's done as soon as possible. And my mudguard!' She gave a little moué of regret, meant to be humorous, but it didn't fool the housekeeper.

'You look pale – quite poorly,' she said with real concern. 'I know your father wouldn't agree with you driving that thing at all.'

'Oh yes, he would, he loved it,' Emma asserted sounding more confident. 'I *would* like a cup of tea though.'

When she was seated in the cosy lounge, with logs set ablaze in the grate, and a lamp shining comfortingly from a rosy shade by a side table, Mrs Cox brought in a silver tray covered by a clean embroidered traycloth bearing familiar family china, and a plate of new baked scones and cakes.

'Put plenty of sugar in,' she said, as she herself poured tea from the pot. 'You don't look well, whatever you say. What's the matter now? Is anything worrying you? If so – I know the master – your dear father would have wanted you to say.'

Not wishing to face the kindly questioning concern on the housekeeper's face, Emma avoided her gaze.

'No. Nothing; – I – I – *really* I'm just a bit tired,' there was a pause before she asked over-casually, 'That letter – the one I was expecting—' Her words trailed off.

'Yes, dear Mrs Bradley, you were saying—'

'Oh, it's nothing. I—'

'But I think it *is*.' The woman's voice assumed sudden firm-ness. 'And I've made up my mind now. You should *know*.'

'Know what?'

'Letters *did* come.' The statement was clear, deliberate, 'but *he* – Mr Arthur, your husband – was here one day, the first time, when the postman brought one. He took the envelope himself, looked at it and put it in his pocket. Then he told me it was someone worrying you – "a business concern" or – or – I don't exactly remember the words. Anyway, he showed it to me again — the writing was very bold, and said, "If you ever receive another of these, I *want* it. Keep it for me. I shall call every Monday and collect such offensive communications. They could be very upsetting", he said. I didn't know what to do, but in the end he was so insistent and almost threatened me. "If I find out you've not carried out my orders", he said, or something like it, "your employment here will end. I will *not* have Mrs Bradley worried—"'

The cold feeling of shock turned slowly to mounting joy and warmth, followed by rising anger.

So it had been Arthur after all, and *not* Evan's neglect. How dare he? Oh how dare he be so maliciously, deceitfully devious. Emma looked up then, her cheeks rose-pink from a conflict of emotions.

'If only you'd said,' she remarked reproachfully. 'If only — but no, I must not blame you, it wasn't your fault; you weren't to know.'

'What, my dear?'

'How very *very* important to me those notes were, and how very dear. Were there many?'

'Just two — until today. Mr Arthur had those. But another came this morning—'

Emma stood up quickly, jerking the tray, and knocking a cup over. Ignoring the stain of liquid down her bodice front, she held out a shaking hand. 'Give it to me, Mrs Cox, I promise you won't suffer for it. Just *give* it to me.'

The agony and frightened, imploring expectancy of the pale young face impelled Mrs Cox to hurry from the room and appear almost immediately with an envelope in her hand.

'This is the last one,' she said, almost pushing it into Emma's grasp. 'I don't know! — I may've been wrong in giving Mr Bradley the others, but the way he said it — that they'd upset you! I didn't want that. I was stupid not to know there must be something funny about the whole thing. I didn't like it; deep down I had doubts, but—' She broke off, shaking her head.

Emma, who'd hardly heard what was said, simply replied

mechnically, 'It's all right. I understand. Don't worry, just — just leave me, Mrs Cox; I want to be alone. This is important.'

'Very well, my dear. Only have your tea. You look quite exhausted to me, not yourself at all.' Her eyes — if Emma had seen and noticed, had a speculative look in them — a dawning knowledge slowing bringing recent past events into focus. The master's daughter was not merely concerned about an old friend, the housekeeper decided, she had all the signs on her of being what was known by fashionable circles as *enceinte*, or in 'an interesting condition'. And if that was so it might explain Mr Arthur's concern. Naturally, he wouldn't want his young wife worried at such a time. But why such secrecy? Hovering about the kitchen and hall, hoping she'd done no harm in producing the letter, Mrs Cox waited for the click of tea-cups or Emma's voice calling her back again. But quite ten minutes passed before she had a summons.

When she entered the lounge Emma was standing with the envelope clutched to one side of her bodice. Her grey eyes were brilliant now; a wild-rose colour flooded her cheeks. The mobile lips trembled slightly, verging between joy and a lingering anxiety. Inner excitement burned like the glow of a lamp about her. For a second or two Mrs Cox was taken aback and slightly afraid. She was a practical woman, not given to excessive moods or imaginings. But there seemed something suddenly *too* intense about the slender figure in dove-grey, confronting her. Why, she was even trembling, the poor child, and beneath a thin froth of lace at her neck, the quick jerking of a pulse betrayed the wild beating of her heart.

'Thank you. Oh, thank you, Mrs Cox,' she heard Emma's voice saying. 'You'll never understand what this means to me, and Arthur needn't know it's come. He *mustn't* — you do see that, don't you? No lies need to be told — there'll be no trouble, ever—' The colour suddenly drained from Emma's face; she swayed slightly and would have fallen if the other woman hadn't caught her and eased her gently back on to a chair.

'Now sit still,' Mrs Cox said. 'Just rest until I give you some-thing—'

'It's all right, I—'

'You do as you're told,' came the short command, 'and don't dare move.' She hurried to the kitchen and quickly returned with something in a glass. Holding it to Emma's lips she said, 'Sal volatile. Better than brandy — in your condition.'

The words didn't register with Emma for quite a minute; then glancing up she asked, almost in a whisper, 'What's that? What did you say, about — about my *condition*?'

'You know very well, my dear. And it's nothing to be ashamed of. Forgive me if I'm wrong. But — you're going to have a baby aren't you?'

'I *think* so,' Emma agreed. 'That's why—'

'What?'

'I don't want people knowing until they have to. There's the paper, you see, and — other things. So please keep quiet, Mrs Cox, I'll be upset and really annoyed if you say anything.' Confidence and something of her old high-spirited manner were already reviving on a wave of optimism through her being. When she stood up after hastily swallowing the liquid, followed by a strong cup of sweet tea, her head had stopped whirling, and her feet were steady.

She looked radiant.

'Now,' she said, 'I'll have to hurry back. I'm late.'

'In that *car*? Is it safe? With you as you are?'

Emma laughed.

'I'm a healthy strong creature in full possession of my normal faculties,' she boasted, 'and I could drive that old thing blindfold.'

'I hope you won't try.' The remark was severe and meant to scold.

'As if I *would*. The only thing is—' There was a doubtful pause.

'Yes?'

'Rosalind — I haven't seen her.'

The housekeeper sighed.

'I wouldn't worry about that. She probably wouldn't notice you at all today. This morning she went into a temper over

something, and if she'd been a normal child I'd have — I'd really
have put her over my knee. But, of course, with Miss Rosalind,
patience is the only thing, and leaving her alone. She's in her
room now, sulking. That poor girl — the governess — takes
endless trouble with her. Sometimes I think she's getting a little
more approachable and reasonable. At others I just wonder
what it will be like when she's older. Still, you've got to hope for
the best; the future's unpredictable, as they say, and you never
know.'

That was true, Emma thought, with a niggle of fear welling
up again — no-one *ever* could tell, quite, what the days ahead
would bring. In her own case, more than Rosalind's, a very
large question mark had risen. What was it Evan wanted to talk
to her about? And what would his reaction be when she told him
about the coming child? Then Arthur! why had he taken such
trouble to interfere with her correspondence? Did he suspect?
But how could he? — she hadn't yet even consulted a doctor. She
couldn't be absolutely *certain*. She *was*, though. Deep down she
was as sure as she'd been of anything in her life, that she was
carrying Evan Lloyd's baby.

In spite of her assertion of lateness, and having to get back to
Eastwood as quickly as possible, she drove by a roundabout
route through the forest, and stopped the car by the ruined
priory, to take out the letter and read it again:

Emma, where the devil are you? and why don't you reply? Is it
some game you're playing with me? If so be honest with me
and say so, so that I can call it a day and push off to the far
east or somewhere. If it hadn't been for a spot of lecturing I
got here that kept me tied every day I'd have been down like a
shot and — what would I have done? — carried you off by the
hair of your head to some benighted place where we could live
off berries? God knows. The point is I need you, I'm mad
about you, you're my obsession, and my dream, if a hard-
boiled, practically penniless adventurer can be said to have a
dream. Anyway that's the way it is. And I hope you feel the
same. We've got to *talk*. I've news it's important for you to

know. Can you meet me in London — St Pancras Station, 12.30 p.m. a week today? You'd better. I'll be there, and if you don't turn up I shall know that either the Bradley odds are stacked too heavily against me, or you've changed your mind and decided after all that Evan Lloyd, Welshman and maybe a bit of an opportunist, isn't a good enough bet to squander your favours on. However, if you *don't* appear, my darling, I shall quite probably arrive on the doorstep of Oaklands or Eastwood unexpectedly, and make one hell of a fuss. So think up a plausible excuse if you have to for getting an early train — I'm sure your nimble mind can manage it. Understand?

Till we meet again then,
Evan.

He gave no address, which was annoying. She'd have liked to scribble an answer and get it into the post straightaway, saying 'I'll be there. However tricky it is, I'll come; Emma.'

But he hadn't given her the chance to refuse. Instead he'd bossily made a statement, which contained also a threat if she didn't comply.

She smiled secretly to herself, knowing she had no alternative but to go along with his plan. A meeting with him at Oaklands would be too dangerous. London was different. From St Pancras they could take a cab or go by underground to some tucked-away little cafe in Chelsea or Soho where they'd be free to talk, safe from prying eyes or malicious conjecturing. She'd drive from Eastwood to Leyford on the pretext of a shopping expedition, catching the early nine-thirty train for the City, which would allow her a brief time to visit the cloakroom, adjust her hat and veil, and see she was looking her best as she walked along the platform for her assignation with Lloyd. Of course, he might be there before her, waiting, as the train puffed in. It didn't matter; she would have comb, powder, rose-balm, and perfume in her reticule, and would see through the mirror of the first class ladies' toilette on the train, that her headgear was tilted at just the right angle, allowing the suspicion of silky fringe to show with one tendril of a curl over her cheek. The night before the exciting event, she'd take a pill containing laudanum, that the doctor had prescribed for her during a period of sleepless nights following her father's death. This would ensure she'd wake refreshed, with her eyes at their very best. Oh, she wanted to be beautiful for Lloyd. After the weeks of waiting he mustn't be disillusioned by his first glimpse of her again.

When the time arrived, everything went to plan and was even easier than she'd anticipated. Arthur had gone out unusually early on some project concerning a new foal. Jonathan was perusing a letter from Lord Wendle in the library when she set off in the car after making a casual statement to her maid about a shopping expedition. She left the vehicle at the nearest country train junction of Winkley from where she caught the train to the City.

It was in her own terms — 'a black and yellow day'. Trees and fields were misty grey under yellowing skies, the windows of her first class carriage damp with steam. Emma was alone in her compartment, with her reticule and a magazine on her lap. She appeared composed, but wasn't. Beneath a new golden-brown cape her heart beat riotously. Though her back was erect, and her perfect profile turned in a steady gaze to the passing land-scape, her slim fingers in their soft brown gloves tapped rest-lessly on the paper. Every few minutes or so a hand strayed automatically to her temple, making sure that except for the single curl, no wanton tendrils of hair spoiled her elegant appearance. It was silly to be so particular, she thought — Evan had once told her she must never try to be sophisticated — he liked her wild and elusive looking as a woodland nymph.

But today was different. The expensive rust and gold outfit — the shining pointed-toed boots peeping beneath the braid trimmed hem of the silk gown, her provocatively tilted hat with its veiling and suggestion of osprey, the tiny gold buttons of her bodice glinting beneath the cape — and the bustle, not too large, but sufficiently so to lend a touch of audacity — all, some-how, made her feel mistress of the situation. She would at first be just a *trifle* aloof when she met Lloyd, then — suddenly, her hands would be in his, and they would be staring with wonder into each other's eyes. They wouldn't kiss, of course, not in public — but later? A smile twitched her mouth as she contemplated the precious time they'd have together.

Once or twice, lost in her wild imaginings, she was aware of figures passing down the corridor, and was careful to appear haughtily aloof, with not the quiver of an eyelash. It was a little unusual even in 1905 for a young woman of 'class' to be travelling alone, and young men could get mistaken ideas and prove troublesome, given the slightest encouragement. No attempt was made, however, to invade her privacy, and when, amid a great deal of puffing, and snorting, and thick whirling coils of smoke, the train drew in to St Pancras, she was able to smooth her skirts and cape effectively, tilt her saucy hat a further half an inch forward, and lifting her gown by one hand, in the other holding her reticule under the cape, stepped down through the door into the bustling crowd.

It was almost impossible at first to distinguish one figure from another — there was so much scuffling, calls for porters, wheeling of trucks, whistles and lights appearing intermittently through the smoke. The air smelled thick, and damp, and foggy. A man in a tall hat bumped into her and asked if he could get her a cab.

'No, no thank you,' Emma answered. 'Someone is meeting me.' The man gave a polite bow, touched his hat and went on.

But where was Evan? Obviously apart from the smoke, London was in the grip of a fog. She could discern ahead in the distance, the blurred shapes of cabs and horses waiting. Supposing Evan had been delayed or was late? Or supposing there'd been a street accident?

With a tiny niggle of panic rising in her she searched the platform, moving towards the gates where the ticket collector stood. There was a restaurant on her left, thank goodness. If all else failed, if something was wrong, she could go in there, have something to eat and then take the first train back again.

But there was no need.

Just as she was wondering what to do, a familiar figure emerged through the yellow light — hatless, and casually dressed, with a muffler round his neck.

Evan!

In her excitement and relief she ran forward, moving too quickly and carelessly. A large man carrying a case banged into her, knocking her precious, carefully arranged hat over one eye, on to her shoulder. She tried to retrieve it, but with the collision all sophistry had vanished. Curls tumbled from their coils and pins. She swept them from her eyes, and forgetting about stupid elegance and fashion, broke into a bubble of laughter, as Evan swept her into his arms.

Convention was forgotten. Passionate and desirous, hungry with longing, they stood there for a few moments locked so tightly together she could hardly breathe.

After that short delicious pause she pulled herself together, and heard him saying, 'A good thing you made it. And stop fiddling with that thing—' He pulled the hat from her hand, and by its ribbons, slung it over his shoulder.

'Evan, you *mustn't*. You can't—'

'Can't I?' She sensed rather than saw the mischievous tilt of his lips. 'Reserve telling me what I can or can't do until later. At the moment you must be hungry. So am I. I know a nice little place in Soho. Come on, we'll go there. I'll get a cab.'

Just as she'd imagined until then, although later things were to turn out very differently.

12

The tricky journey through London streets in the thickening fog
was too uncertain — too confused by muffled sounds of rattling
wheels, car horns, horses' hooves and shouting, for talk of plans
or intimate conversation; but the warm strength of Evan's
hand, his other tightly encasing her waist, was sufficient assurance to her that the bond between them had increased rather
than waned.

The restaurant, L'Oiseau d'Or, was tucked away in a discreet
Soho corner frequented mostly by artists and writers. Lace and
gauze curtains obscured daylight to a mere glimmer, but inside
rose-shaded lamps cast intriguing shadow-play over pannelled
walls. Waiters moved soundlessly on thick-carpeted floors,
treading their ways past small intimate tables — in and out of
alcoves, carrying trays or gilt-embossed menu cards. Prices were
comparatively reasonable, yet an air of luxury and secret excitement pervaded the atmosphere, intensified by the aroma of
wines, tobacco smoke, mostly of Turkish origin, and feminine
perfume suggesting intrigue and glamour.

The clientele was of a varied character, including one or two
extravagantly clad elderly women hoping beneath their painted
exteriors for a harmless touch of youth's lost romance — couples
on the brink of amorous adventure, and the merely bored and
sophisticated, savouring the best brandy and liqueurs, with
watchful sardonic amusement; English, French, Italian —
colourful continentals — all were there; but there was no
ribaldry; no sound above muted conversation and laughter on a
low key, except for the faint strains of a violin being played in a
recess at the far end of the room.

Evan and Emma were conducted to a small table cunningly

shielded from public view by a bead curtain and wine was ordered, followed by a choice of entrées.

There was a pause until glasses were deposited before them, then, with their eyes riveted magnetically on each other's, Evan said, 'Now, I suppose, the story must be told.'

'Story?' she echoed, ineffectually.

'Or stories,' he added quickly, 'yours and mine; and how we — how we're going to deal with it all.' This wasn't quite what she'd expected. Actually she'd thought of nothing concisely — only joy of meeting him, of them being together again, and of the important news about the baby. But, of course, there was much more to explain, and tearing her gaze from his, she said in soft hurried tones, 'I never had your letters, Evan, until the last one. They — *he* — stopped them. So you see it wasn't my fault you had no answer.'

'Bradley you mean? That rotten—?' The flame of indignation burned his face.

She nodded. 'He intercepted them. But don't let's talk about him — I've something—'

He leaned forward, and stretching one arm, clasped her nearby hand in a tight grip, at the same moment interrupting what she'd so wanted to say. 'Listen, Emma darling, let me make things clear first then we can go on from there. There's a lot you know about me already — that I want you and care for you more than I have for any other woman in my life. That's the one thing that will never change, *cariad*. So for God's — no, not for God's — for both of us, you and me — try and understand the rest.'

Her heart sank a little.

'Go on, tell me then.'

'I've got to leave you for a time,' he continued, watching her intently, noting a little of the colour leave her face, and her eyes narrow under their fringes of dark lashes.

'*Leave* me? Again? For how long?'

'A year.'

'A year? But *why*? — when—?'

'Circumstance,' he told her. 'I've mentioned before that there was a good deal in my life you didn't know about. Well — for that matter we haven't known each other long, have we? Not comparatively, although I can't imagine now any worthwhile existence without you. But it has to be, Emma. If it was practical, I'd say come with me, fling your cap over the windmill and let's stay together. But it wouldn't work. This is a one-man job—'

'I see.' Even in her own ears her voice sounded shrill and high, a hard, mechanical squeak.

'No you damn well don't; why should you? Africa's only half the story.'

'*Africa?*'

'I've been offered a twelve-month teaching job in quite a go-ahead new college. Life will be pretty primitive, I suppose, and a woman wouldn't be welcome. I have to be free, without responsibilities of a domestic kind — and it'll be hard going. But I'll manage — on my own. I've *got* to. After that I shall be back with all I need to start our life together — that is — if you want to still.'

She was confounded. How *could* he sit there and so cold-bloodedly inform her that he wouldn't see her again for a whole year? In that one agonising moment of revelation all thought of telling him about the coming child was resolutely extinguished. He was *leaving* her — had *planned* to, while all the time she'd fretted and longed for a sight of him — just a word assuring her of his love and determination to guide her through the difficult months ahead.

Now, *Africa.*

Contempt of her own naiveté, her romantic stupid belief in him compelled her to say bitterly, 'I *quite* understand, Evan. And if that's what you wanted to tell me, I think we should finish the conversation, don't you?' She looked at her watch, while cold, unreal words left her lips. 'It's been nice seeing you, of course, but I *am* busy, and I'd like to catch the first train back—' She tried to get to her feet, but her dress caught, and a hand knocked a glass of wine over, spilling the remains of golden liquid down the white tablecloth.

'Sit *down*,' Lloyd told her, through his teeth. 'I've not finished yet, not by a long chalk. And there's no need to make a scene. Look, the waiter's coming.'

White-lipped, she adjusted her gown and once more seated herself rigidly on the chair.

When the waiter had mopped the wine up and taken the glass away, Evan said bluntly, 'You didn't know, of course, and you never asked, so I put off giving the information until I was sure of you – or thought so. The truth is, Emma, I'm married. I have a wife.'

'A *wife*?'

'Now don't look like that. Not in the way you think, not—'

'Then in what way? What other way is there? If you're married.'

In sarcastic tones he said drily, 'You should know.'

He flinched.

She waited. 'Well?'

'Do you want me to go on?'

'You may as well.' Shock had momentarily dimmed pain; all she felt was a wild kind of anger and shame.

'It all happened years ago. Eight, to be precise, when I was at College. I went over to Ireland during a vacation, on a walking tour. It was early summer. I found digs at a small place in the mountains that was all romantic, very Celtic, full of beauty and blarney – unreal somehow – like Wales in a way but with a difference. There were ruined castles and rivers, and cross-roads where they danced the Kerry Dance. There were black-shawled bent old women – very tiny, looking like pixies, and luscious black-eyed colleens with laughter that had music in it. Oh yes, it was an enchanted holiday, and one weekend there was a fair. It was then I met the girl – Shirin is her name, Shirin Kathleen O'Malley. She was the daughter of a schoolmaster – a grim hardworking underpaid disciplinarian who kept a watch on her as well as he could. But that night she managed to be free, and later – when the fun and games were over, we – the inevitable happened, as it sometimes does, between a lovely girl – and believe me, she was quite a beauty, curling black hair, rose-red lips and cheeks and the bluest eyes you ever saw — and a fellow like me. It wasn't planned, I was infatuated, briefly, but that was all. Unfortunately there were consequences. Some weeks after returning to Wales I heard from her that she was pregnant.'

'Oh.'

He didn't look at her, as he continued, 'I didn't doubt that I was the father. She'd been virgin till I came along. A second letter arrived from the father, censorious, vituperative, then more conciliatory when he informed me that he naturally expected and trusted me to do the honourable thing and return as soon as possible to Ireland and marry her. Which I did.'

Still no word came from Emma's lips.

'It was a fiasco from the start, of course,' Evan went on. 'I had no money, we had no interests in common. It was expected I would find something to do in the vicinity and make my way while we spent our days together with her father and his sister. She was a kindly but depressed kind of woman who'd done her best to bring up the little girl Shirin after her mother died when she was only two. I learned the reason for the woman's gloom — partially — only a month or two later following an unwarranted attack of temper from my young wife when she threatened me with a knife. There was a taint apparently in the family on her mother's side, and obviously Shirin had inherited it.'

'Is that all?'

'No. Shirin had a baby that died at birth — mercifully. I can see that now. But at the time things were worse; she, my wife, never recovered. I took various jobs in the meantime, and eventually left for Wales. All through the following years I've managed somehow, to contribute to her keep. But last month I heard the schoolmaster had died, leaving his sister practically nothing financially, with Shirin dependent on her. She's in a home now, completely mentally sick with no hope given for her recovery. The place is quite pleasant, but in future the cost for part of her board has to be paid. That's why I'm going to Africa. The post is a very rewarding one financially and whatever my faults, I *do* feel I've a certain duty to give what I can. If she'd no-one of her own to help. other sources or authorities would pay up I guess. But I'm her husband, by law, still. Divorce is out of the question so far. She's Catholic anyway. But soon, Emma, I'm seeing a solicitor about having proof of her insanity. In this country I believe a marriage *can* be annulled under certain circumstances. Until then—' His eyes searched her face intently, imploringly. 'Oh darling – can't you bear with me, and try, at least *try* to understand? A year apart, and then – oh hell! – if the legal business can't be gone through, we can at least be together. Isn't love the important thing?'

Recklessly Emma replied, 'I *thought* so. *Now* I'm wondering.'

'My God, you're a cold one,' he said bitterly.

She ignored his outburst. 'Why didn't you tell me before – about being married?'

'You mean I should have gone around wearing a placard saying, "I'm married, I've got a wife, so don't touch me"?'

'How ridiculous.'

'And how insensitive of you going on like this, determined not to understand.'

'Oh I *do*,' she snapped airily, hating herself for her facade of hardness, of sarcasm that was unlike her. 'Only too well. You've cared for me, yes – when it suited you. You've been—'

'Faithful to thee, Cynara, in my fashion,' he quoted. 'Oh well, that's it I suppose, if you're so dead set on putting the wrong interpretation on things. I know *one* thing though—' He paused, staring at her so fixedly she had to steel herself not to soften, or to blurt out the truth allowing the tears to flood her eyes, as she confessed all that was in her heart.

'Yes?' she said stonily. 'Go on.'

'We'll never be free of each other, Emma, not while we both live. *I* know it, and so do you. And I shall come back – one day when you discover what you've missed. I only hope it's not too late.'

She gave a light laugh meaning nothing. 'For what?'

He didn't reply.

The waiter, with tempting-looking omelettes with foreign names, smelling tastily savoury, came to the table. Both ate mechanically, Emma, only just contriving to swallow hers. It tasted like sawdust. Their conversation following was practical, dealing with trivialities that passed emptily like a scene in a play.

In another half hour the nightmare was over. They left, side by side, uncommunicative and miserable. In the cab taking Emma to the station, Lloyd made an effort to break the deadlock, but her mind was still too frozen to meet him halfway. The fog by then was a yellow blanket, and they only reached St Pancras in the nick of time to catch the early train back to Leyford. Evan helped her into the carriage. Thick coils of yellow smoke drifted past the window. Before he closed the door he grasped her hand suddenly, and pulled her tempestuously towards him. 'Don't go, Emma,' he said urgently. 'There's another train in two hours – don't – *please*—'

He tried to pull her out. It was no use.

There was a whistle; he stepped back on to the platform.

'I shall write,' he shouted, before the rhythm of the engine jerked the train forward, slowly at first, then with ever increasing speed. 'Leyford – post restante. Take care of yourself—'

The tears filled her eyes then, even his were bright. But neither saw. Her head under its absurd hat quickly became a mere intermittent shape receding into the distance, and his a vanishing blob through the uncertain blur of smoke and fog.

He stood watching until the serpent-like puffing form had finally disappeared, then turned and walked away on heavy feet.

Emma adjusted her cape and bustle in a corner seat of the carriage. An elderly man from the opposite side gave a brief glance over his paper then looked down again. He was mildly curious, sensing a lovers' tiff. Perhaps, during his scanning of the *Times* business columns a faint envy stirred him for the lost days of youth's vagaries. But presently only the train's steady rhythm registered.

Emma felt nothing at all but desolation and an emptiness worse at the time, than a forecast of death.

How could she get through the days ahead? She had no faith

in Evan's promise to write, or in any possibility of any mutual future. Most probably they would never meet again.

'Never — never—' the great mechanical wheels thudded as a changing vista of scenery passed by — fields, trees and grey villages huddled under a yellowing sky. It was all over.

Everything.

Then suddenly she felt sick, and remembered.

The child. The fruit of her love and Evan's — it would be born without his even knowing of its existence.

A Bradley.

Gradually the significance of the situation revolved into tormented reality. Arthur would have to know. Unless—.

For a second she toyed with the idea of an abortion, but as quickly abandoned it. She just couldn't resort to such bitter destruction.

Anyway — her mouth held a momentary sardonic twist — Jonathan would doubtless be pleased, and his pleasure would react on her husband very favourably. That Arthur's presumed son — and she felt strongly the baby would be a boy — was a bastard, wouldn't worry her husband at all. Perhaps he would not resent it, so long as no one ever knew about it. If they *did* — she shivered as she remembered his threats and the little horse whip in the cupboard.

Oh God! what had she gone into?

Panic for a few moments swamped all other emotions in her; but presently it subsided, leaving her curiously calm and bereft of all feeling.

It was evening when she reached Eastwood. No-one except a housemaid appeared to be about. She went upstairs immediately, changed, washed, and used more lip salve and makeup than usual.

When she went down to dinner later Arthur was already seated by the fire with the decanter and brandy and soda in front of him on the small table.

The firelight gave his fair hair a golden sheen. His blue eyes held a brilliance of sun on frozen water. No Greek god or legendary knight could have looked more handsome.

'Ah!' he said, half rising, then seating himself again. 'My wife. How very beautiful you look, my dear.'

Emma smiled.

'Thank you, Arthur.'

She'd taken pains with her appearance, because she knew now the best thing for her peace of mind, was to tell him about the baby, and get it over as quickly as possible, and that she must use a little flattery and beguilement, looking as ravishing as possible.

The silver-grey gown sprinkled with diamanté suited her fey, almost fairy-like appearance. The lip salve added both seduction and sophistry. In her hair a single white bloom from the conservatory glowed like a pale star against the molten coils of glistening hair. Round the pale column of her throat above the creamy shoulders, she wore a necklace of pearls given to her by Arthur as a wedding gift.

'A new dress?' he enquired. 'The result of your — shopping spree?' So he'd heard. They'd informed him at the stables, of course, before her maid did.

'No,' she replied. 'I didn't buy much after all. You've seen this before — at that important dance. Remember?'

'Ah, yes,' he agreed in a rather thick voice. He didn't, of course, he was already befuddled by too much liquor. But for once this only made matters easier, and later that night, when they'd retired to bed, he accepted her news of the pregnancy almost laconically, with far more tolerance than she'd believed possible.

'How very interesting,' he said, running a finger down her neck and one white breast. 'You have, then, been enjoying yourself quite a lot in your old-fashioned way, dearest?'

Steeling herself to an airy shows of light bravado, she bluffed, 'If you remember you suggested, or gave me permission first, to have a little life of my own. Otherwise, of course, I wouldn't have dared.' There was a pause in which she held her breath, then he said. 'That's true. Quite true. I take it, though, I'm entitled to know my — substitute's name? Though perhaps I can guess it—'

'I'm sure it's better not,' she said firmly. 'Unless you wish the child to be called by it, when he's born. But you wouldn't, would you? After all, it's what your father wants, isn't it? — Another Bradley in the family?'

'You're very clever, Emma. Yes, I agree.' After a further short silence, he continued reflectively, almost in a whisper, '—Bradley. Yes — a *Bradley*.'

Suddenly his hands were about her breasts, thighs and buttocks, his lips hot on her flesh, and he was ravishing her in a way she found particularly revolting.

'That seals it then,' he said at last, in smug satisfied tones, 'and I've never had to use the whip. You really *are* quite a gem of a wife, Emma. And tomorrow we'll tell my father.'

Exhausted, sick with humiliation, Emma lay rigidly beside him, sleepless until the morning.

After breakfast, Jonathan heard the news and was more than delighted — exuberant.

For a brief time, Emma wished she could die — until she remembered the living entity within her that was also Evan's, and later, the weekly *Woman's Post*.

Such things were *real*, and for the future.

She had to go on.

13

Emma had one short note from Evan before he sailed for Africa, and this was post-marked Ireland. It was waiting for her at Leyford General Post Office when she called, and the contents bore no address, just a brief communication saying:

Dearest stubborn Emma, I'm here, in this country of Kelpies and blue-eyed colleens. The air is balmy, mild, damp and empty. Empty without you; but I'm not going to dwell on romanticism and sentimental yearnings. That's for my verse-scribbling — such as it is. At heart I'm a realist able to face facts, as you are, though you don't admit it. If you weren't, we'd be no earthly use to each other. So don't fret and pine. A year isn't all that long, and though I detest the thought of your having to put up with A.B., I tell myself you've got all that it takes to keep him under control. Jonathan isn't a bad fellow beneath his bossy airs and ambitions. He may be devious, but there are no flies on him, he can see straight, and I'm sure would stick up for you in a crisis. So if anything worries you, turn to him. He'll see you through, and I mean that, however much I detest him.

Well, that's about all, I think. Words are just padding in a case like this. In the next week, after I've settled things here, I shall be sailing for Africa. Wish me luck.

As ever yours,
My love, Evan.

There was a postscript. 'Shirin is worse. It was a good thing I came. I'm more than ever certain it was the only thing for me to do.'

After a dull feeling of disappointment followed by a sense of frustration at the matter-of-fact tone of the letter, Emma tore it up, and put the pieces of paper into her reticule. She didn't want advice over her own life, or references to Shirin. That she existed at all as Evan's wife was still a shock to her. It wasn't the girl's fault, of course. If Evan had been more controlled, with any sense of discipline in him those years ago, his doomed marriage would never have taken place. In her loneliness she blamed him bitterly for the past. There were times when she felt acute resentment for his invasion into her life. He hadn't been free, even during their first passionate love-making. If he'd told her he had a wife she wouldn't have given him a second thought.

Or would she?

How could anyone say what *might* have been? Life could be so unpredictable and cruel. Her own marriage to Arthur had proved this. She'd married him believing their existence together would have glamour, security, and the power to further her father's ambition for the *Echo*.

But instead? At such a point she stifled her imagination, bringing facts ruthlessly into place. There were twelve long months ahead of her without Evan, a period in which anything might happen. What? No-one could tell, except for one thing. The birth of her baby — if all went well; and before that, endless days which she must see were not wasted. Oaklands still remained, and the newly launched *Woman's Post*. These were facets of her life peculiarly and individually her own. The knowledge fortified her. Sometimes it was as though she heard her loved father saying, 'You'll come through, Emma, hold on, love, everything will be all right in the end.' And it wasn't only imagination, she knew that. Something of him — of his genes — ran strong in her blood. She was a Fairley. This was her heritage, what she had to cling to.

*

Jonathan's elation concerning Emma's condition was so jubilant the whole household of Eastwood soon knew of it. There was a new feeling about the place. Good will and excitement combined with increasing optimism about his political future created a sense of bonhomie to which even Amelia responded, by refraining from her sessions of private tonic-taking, and evoking a load of kindly advice and tips to the expectant mother – old-fashioned many of them, but some of real help, for which Emma was grateful.

'You really *should* take a bit more rest now, love,' Amelia said one day, quite fondly. 'Not lie about all day like some do – but try to be a bit more placid. Stop driving that rickety old motor-car so much. I never liked those new-fangled things, and I reckon it's too late in life now to get used to them. But why don't we take a carriage trip together, you and me, and have a right good shopping spree? There's new clothes you'll be needing, and a French shop's opened for baby things in that Arcade place off High Street. We could have tea out, or a nip of sherry in Bartons. All the high-class folk go there. Jonathan'd like it. He's very fussy now about us appearing among the right people, and I'd be extra careful to talk right.'

She was so enthusiastic, so flushed at the prospect, that Emma couldn't help smiling, and agreeing.

'Yes. I'd like that. All right, we will.'

'Good. I allus say a change is as good as a – tonic – do they call it?' She laughed heartily. 'That's a joke. Anyway, my love, I can promise you you'll have no need to be ashamed of me. Not like that son of mine.' A shadow briefly crossed her face.

Emma felt a pang.

'I'm sure Arthur's not *ashamed*. Don't think such stupid things. You imagine too much.'

'No, my dear,' Amelia's voice sounded uncharacteristically firm. 'It's not imagination. I know where I stand. With Jonathan, too, though not so much. He treats me right, does what he can for me. Allus has. And at heart he's a good man. I hope he gets what he's aiming for, that's all.'

So did Emma.

The election so far didn't seem imminent, but at Westminster rivalry between the two chief parties was increasing, with the odds strengthening in Liberal favour. It was by then evident that women were becoming restive and wanting a share of management in the country's affairs. In 1870 a bill to give women the vote had successfully passed a second reading in the House, but in the years following had failed to become law. In 1903 Emmeline Pankhurst and her daughter had taken up the challenge and organised a group of women represented by all classes, to carry on the campaign. No major political party was in favour, but Jonathan, frequently one step ahead in foreseeing the trend of future events, was careful in currying favour with the feminine members of the constituency he was determined to represent. He worked untiringly, yet with a subtlety his daughter-in-law would not previously have thought him capable of. During the spring and summer months of the current year, he was helped unconsciously by Emma, who pushed *Woman's Post* into becoming, on its own account, a popular weekly.

Regarding herself one day through her mirror after returning to Eastwood from a particularly full and tiring day in Charbrook, she noted, with dismay that her face was thinner; emphasising the darkening rings under her eyes. She was wearing deep olive green that intensified her unusually pale skin and luxuriant copper-beech tones of her hair. But she looked older; no longer the radiant girl her father had known and loved. Something of her vivid tempestuous quality seemed to have been drained from her, replaced by a young matron of purpose who was already scheduled in certain circles as the 'new woman'.

Arthur, who came into the bedroom some minutes later must have noticed. After glancing at her, he said, 'Charbrook again, I suppose? Isn't it time you gave a little more thought to your appearance? These days you don't appear exactly ravishing, my dear.'

'I don't intend to,' she answered shortly. 'And I didn't ask you to come in here just at this moment before I've even taken off my hat, or washed and changed.'

'No indeed,' he said mockingly. 'A thousand apologies. I'd forgotten I had to have permission to enter the connubial bedchamber.'

'Oh, don't be so silly.'

With a sudden tug he jerked a pin from her hat, and pulled it off. She put a hand up as a rich coil of curls fell loose to her shoulder. 'What's the matter with you? Don't, Arthur—'

'Don't, *don't*!' he echoed in mincing high tones. 'It's always the same nowadays, isn't it? "Don't do this, Arthur, don't do that. Don't — don't — or I'll tell your papa". Oh I know you've got him under control, now his beloved heir-to-be is safely thriving in your plump little belly — pardon me, my love, I don't mean to be offensive.' He strolled over to her, put a hard arm round her shoulders, and pulled her round fiercely to face him. Her mouth was coldly set, her grey eyes — narrowed under their thick dark lashes as he jerked her chin upwards and said in the threatening way he used when he'd drunk too much '—But he isn't that by rights, is he? The bastard you're carrying? There's not a streak of Bradley blood in him. *I* know it, and you know it. So far the pater doesn't. But you should be careful, my dear. He'd take it badly — very badly indeed — to learn you'd delivered a by-blow into the family bosom.'

Her cheeks paled. She felt suddenly sick.

His manner changed quickly.

'Now sit down and behave.' He pushed her on to the bed. She was trembling, but forced herself to obey. With his cold eyes staring down on her, hard and brilliant as bright glass, he brought a hand sharp against her face, then jerked open her bodice and ripped it down the front. Following this he removed camisole, skirt and petticoats, and the rest of her undergarments, until she was quite naked. 'Now get up.'

Rigid, repulsed, with a slow creeping fear in her she didn't at first comply. It was only when she saw his glance stray to the cupboard where he kept the hated whip that she got to her feet.

He smiled maliciously. 'Ah! — that's better.' He touched a side of her stomach with the tips of two fingers almost caressingly. 'Poor little blighter,' he said in soft tones, almost a whisper. 'I hope he goes to hell. And you too,' he added after a short pause, 'bitch.'

She made a movement to rise. He bent down, picked up the

clothes and threw them across the room in a bundle. 'Now dress properly, wife dear — something ravishing that will tickle Wendle's fancy and make the old boy really envious. He's coming to dinner, remember? And the dear pater would be disappointed if you didn't appear your most beautiful whore-ish best. The scarlet silk, I think, showing too much bosom, with too many drapes at your intriguing behind. And for God's sake smile—'

No movement touched the hard lines of her lips. He came close again and took her once more by the bare shoulders. 'I said smile — *damn* you — or I'll give you the thrashing of your unholy sweet life—'

Mechanically her mouth stretched from side to side, revealing the white glint of pearly teeth.

With a sigh, he turned away. After a moment, when the crisis had passed, she reached for a wrap and pulled it round her body. He walked heavily to the door, paused there, and looked back before leaving. There was no pain on her face, except a lingering redness where his hard hand had struck her — only contempt and hatred.

Following his burst of temper his nerves quickened. 'Sorry if I was — rather heavy-handed,' he mumbled. 'It isn't easy — things being as they are, and *you*! — if it was *my* child it'd be different.'

'Don't make excuses,' she said, 'or try to explain. And don't ever behave or speak to me like that again, Arthur. If you do, I'll tell your father *everything* — not excusing you at all. I'll even go to a specialist or the Law; I'll expose you, I swear it. Maybe I ought to, anyway. Because you're mad — *mad*.' She paused breathlessly, while he put his hands to his forehead. When he glanced at her again, his handsome face was ravaged. 'Very well, madam. It's a bargain. Quits, if you like.'

He gave the semblance of a sardonic smile, and a second or two later the door slammed and he was gone.

It was only then, after he'd gone, that she relaxed weakly, and as the quick racing of her heart faded, fainted.

After this latest incident, Emma insisted in having the large bedroom that had been so sumptuously furnished for their marriage to herself. Arthur retired to his bachelor apartment; and no questions were asked. Emma was careful to admit in the presence of Amelia and Jonathan that she slept badly, and needed privacy both at night and in the daytime, to rest when she felt like it. Jonathan accepted the explanation for separate rooms. He supposed it was often a usual state of affairs during a woman's pregnancy. Amelia, simple in some ways, was more shrewd in others.

'I don't want to criticise, my dear,' she said one day to Emma, 'heaven knows I've no right. But don't you think the time's coming when you ought to give up going so much to Charbrook? Jolting about can't be all that good for you when you're expecting a baby, and then there's the Dower House. The renovations are almost done now. I don't want you to leave here, but if you and Arthur are going to settle down there before autumn and winter set in, I should have thought you'd want to have a go at making things pretty—' Her voice wavered off haltingly, her plump prettyish face had a frown on it.

'There's plenty of time yet,' Emma said, now hating the thought of moving anywhere with Arthur to be on their own. 'And I do often call on my way back from Oaklands. As for driving harming me—' she laughed, a rather brittle sound, 'I'm strong as an ox. Don't *worry*, Amelia. I couldn't stick being cooped up and cosseted here all the time, or measuring carpets and curtains at that place—'

'That place? What do you mean? Don't you like it any more?'

Emma sighed. 'I don't know. I mean, yes, I suppose so. Of course. Only don't *press* me about it. I'm not myself always these days. I have to get away to – to—' She broke off, wishing Amelia would leave. How could she explain? How could they even possibly talk together with such a secret between them? The great tormented gap of her passion for Evan which still lingered beneath the 'don't care' facade?

The truth would only seem treachery to Arthur's mother. She just had to go on as she was, living a lie until Evan returned to make things right.

If he *could*, and wanted to.

If he *did* return.

The conversation between the two women ended there, and Emma tried to put all thought of the future behind. Each day was lived by her energetically, with a sense of cold purpose for the *Echo*, and disregard for Amelia's fussing and Jonathan's intermittent fits of proprietary concern. His pride in her frequently made her feel traitorous. She wished wholeheartedly at times that the coming child could have been Arthur's. Not the Arthur she knew — the unpredictable warped character who delighted in taunting her whenever possible by snide remarks and sly looks, but the charming stranger she'd first met, the handsome character who'd appeared in the beginning so courteous and friendly. Yes; as a friend she might really have grown to love him in time — not with the devouring passion Evan had woken in her, but in an easy warm way that could have made of their union a successful and rewarding partnership. Now she had to recognise there could never be anything between them but dislike, and on her side contempt.

She did her best in public to hide the latter emotion and Jonathan was deceived, but not Arthur himself. He kept away from her as much as possible, making more frequent visits to David and his mother; but Emma's enmity rankled. Wounded pride and frustrated anger forced him into drinking more heavily as spring passed into summer. His father, away from the house so much, either visiting Lord Wendle or wooing popularity both in the countryside and Leyford itself, was unaware how rapidly a bad habit was quickly becoming a vice. Amelia knew, and tried to reason with him, to no avail.

'What a saint you're becoming at a late date, Mama,' Arthur remarked sarcastically once. 'The kettle calling the pot black, eh?' He laughed derisively, 'Or is it the other way round? — I don't care a bloody damn anyway. Mind your own business—'

He strode away to the stables, leaving Amelia shaken, with tears brimming in her eyes and spilling down her plump cheeks ineffectually.

Eventually Emma accepted that driving regularly to Charbrook had to be curtailed. She continued working on the

editorial side of *Woman's Post* at Eastwood, and found slightly
to her chagrin, that her presence at the offices was not missed
unduly. The supplement had already been listed as a magazine
in its own right, independent of the weekly *Echo*; a certain
public was assured. In one way she had achieved her aim. The
Fairley name still stood for something.

Her baby was born at the end of July — a healthy boy who
gave the minimum of trouble coming into the world. At first he
bore a striking resemblance to Emma, having small features,
blue eyes quickly changing to grey, and a tuft of fair hair that
was to become brown later.

Jonathan was delighted. 'A true Bradley,' he commented in
admiring tones. 'Just like his father, by gum!' The North
Country expression slipped out unknowingly.

Emma, smiling secretly to herself, didn't correct him — she
knew so differently, and anyway it was pleasant that Jonathan
should find so much gratification — however brief the illusion
was to be — in the scrap of humanity lying in her arms.

He was named 'Jon Uldene Bradley' at her specific request —
Jon to mollify Jonathan, who'd expected Arthur to be
included, 'Uldene' because the vicinity of the ruined priory in
the forest had been such a favourite place of hers when she was
a child, and also of her father's. If she'd been free to do so her
choice would have been William Evan, but as matters were,
she realised that Arthur's suspicious mind would instantly seize
on the truth, placing Lloyd in what could be a dangerous
position. He tried hard to make her confirm the name of her
lover, had even sneeringly mentioned Evan's name. But she'd
admitted nothing; had been devious herself even — which was
not a characteristic of hers — in diverting his attention to other
possible sources. Deep down Arthur might know. But he would
never hear it from her lips.

That summer was an achingly beautiful one, bringing lush
thick carpets of bluebells to the forest, frothing clumps of white
blossom foaming along hedgerows, and varying shades of green
to trees where oak merged with silver birch, chestnut, and sycamore.

The Mercedes now was abandoned by Emma, but occasionally she got the man to drive her by carriage, to Oaklands, taking young Jon with her. Once there her spirits lifted. She felt relaxed, free, at home. The scents, sounds, and atmosphere of the forest revitalised and spread a warm glow of enchantment about her. During those rare hours, bitterness against Evan and blame for his departure, turned to a sad but understanding acceptance. She'd received no note from him since he'd sailed for Africa, but then travel by sea took a long time. Often, she knew, letters were lost. She made herself believe something of this had happened, and that one day, any time now, she'd have news.

Meanwhile Jonathan intensified his political campaign through the country, and in December that year of 1905, the Conservative administration resigned, and Campbell Bannerman formed an interim Liberal government.

Jonathan knew then that his subtle dual policies had been justified. Quite soon it was made known that a general election would be held in January 1906.

It was during the following weeks, therefore, before Christmas, that Bradley's first great challenge had to be faced both personally and politically.

But before the issue was resolved something extremely unpleasant and tragic happened at Eastwood.

*

Jessie had returned from boarding school in September. In appearance she had fined down a little, though she would never be a beauty, or what could honestly be termed as good-looking. Nevertheless, her directness, honesty, and straight clear gaze of her blue eyes under thick fair lashes, had an appeal for country folk. She had 'no side' as they said, and was always natural and the same with everyone she met, from lord to stable-boy. To his surprise, Jonathan found her quite an asset in his campaign. She displayed an astute knowledge of politics, which, though demonstrating a touch of a rebel in her, was useful in bridging misunderstandings that might have lost him a following in more radical quarters.

'I wish Arthur was more like you,' Jonathan told her one day, still wondering at the change in her during the last twelve months. 'You should have been a boy.'

Jessie shrugged. 'Perhaps. But because I'm a girl doesn't mean I'm an idiot. Women *ought* to have more of a share in the country's affairs.'

'Now you're talking like one of those "new women",' Jonathan told her a trifle censoriously. 'Don't think along lines like that. Woman's place first of all is in the home, making a happy life for a husband and children.'

'*All* women don't want to get married,' Jessie pointed out. 'They're as capable as men of having careers, given a chance.'

'Been reading about the cranky lot led by that woman Emmeline Pankhurst, have you?' Jonathan's voice was stern. 'Well, forget it, my girl. Nothing will come of it. All they'll get in the end is to fade out as a laughing stock, or land up in prison. So watch your step. And don't scoff at marriage. There'll be a chance coming along — and not too far off, I hope — for you to make a good match. I hope so. I want more grandchildren. The way Arthur and Emma are carrying on doesn't appear very satisfactory to me. Their boy's a fine child, but one isn't enough.'

'Be thankful you have him, anyway,' Jessie said cryptically. 'Jon Uldene!' she laughed. 'I bet Arthur wasn't pleased. *Uldene!* Just fancy.'

'Yes. I agree. But once Emma's made up her mind she won't budge. Like the Dower House — it's all ready, waiting. Yet she makes no move to go there. It's as though she's frightened or something.'

'Perhaps she is,' Jessie spoke laconically, but Jonathan glanced at her sharply, saying, 'What do you mean?'

Jessie shrugged. 'I'm not sure. But there's something about Arthur that would give me the willies if *I* were his wife. He's nearly always half-seas over anyway.'

After a pause, Jonathan said moodily, 'I think you're wrong.

I've pointed out already to him that he was getting too free with the bottle. Lately I thought he'd taken my advice. I hoped so.'

'I should watch him and find out for yourself,' Jessie remarked. 'For your own sake you don't want people talking at this point.'

Jonathan's brows lifted in mild surprise. 'You're becoming a very observant young woman,' he said. 'Practical, too. But don't overdo it. Remember young men like feminine girls.'

'Young men really don't interest me very much,' his daughter re-affirmed flatly, adding with one of her rare attempts at humour, 'Maybe *I* should put up for Parliament, too. Would you appreciate having a daughter appear in the House of Commons as the first female MP ever? It would be something, wouldn't it? A woman making laws instead of babies?'

Jonathan smiled, pretending to be amused; but he wasn't. Banter on such an unlikely topic didn't interest him, although Jessie's reference to Arthur did. Without admitting it, even to himself, concern over his son's increasing tendency to alcoholism already troubled him in his rare leisure moments, and a few evenings following the brief conversation his worst fears were proved.

*

Twilight was slowly deepening over the countryside when Arthur on his way from the Hungry Man, a somewhat bawdy inn on the outskirts of Market Hoe, a village only a few miles from Eastwood, rode the gelding tipsily along the side drive of the house towards the stables. He was seated lop-sided in the saddle, head slumped forward, and was obviously quite drunk. In his free hand he waved a bottle, putting it to his mouth at intervals, then breaking into unintelligible muttering, followed by a brief attempt at a song.

There was no-one at the stables, and as he passed the rear of the house all else was quiet; most of the servants had been given an evening off to go to the local fair. His mount, unsettled and restless at such unpredictable behaviour, reared once or twice. Arthur brought the whip sharply against flanks and neck, and on they went — past rose-gardens and an ornamental pool, lurching shadowed shapes throwing a macabre pattern over the lane from a watery rising moon.

From an upstairs window a square of light showed. It blinked once like a watchful eye, then all was blank and dimmed again. A moment later the horse neighed shrilly, startled by a sudden roar of sound from its rider. Arthur, swearing, dealt it a further savage blow with his crop. The animal reared, throwing its tormentor. For a second or two Arthur was dragged in a stirrup by one boot, then freed. The horse galloped ahead to the stables, leaving Arthur shocked but comparatively unhurt on the ground. Moments later he heaved himself up and stood swaying from side to side, one hand rubbing the back of his head. A trickle of blood oozed between his fingers, but the impact had steadied his senses, and restored an awareness of reality.

He was making his way along a side path past the pool, towards a door which led into the house through a conservatory, when Jonathan's figure suddenly appeared before him — a furious figure of condemnation taking shape from the shadows of a drooping willow tree. ·

'What the hell do you think you're doing?' he growled, grasping his son by the tumbled neckscarf, 'What are you playing at, eh? — *eh?*' He shook the startled figure mercilessly, until Arthur's face was crimson and gasping. 'Determined to make a scandal are you? — a mockery of all I've done for you? My ambitions — all my plans and hopes—'

'Oh damn your bloody ambitions,' Arthur managed to shout as the relentless hard hand released him. 'Leave me alone, blast you! What d'you care about *me*? Nothing — *nothing!*' he spat crudely, waved an arm and would have pushed past Jonathan, but his father was too quick and brought a fist hard against the younger man's face. Arthur reeled for a second, then recovered, and started laughing, a mocking jarring sound of undiluted contempt.

'Don't try your bullying ways on *me*, papa,' he said sneeringly. 'If it comes to a punch-up, I'm a better man anyway. Go

on, get out of my way. Leave me in peace for God's sake, or
you'll be the laughing stock of the neighbourhood.' He took a
step backwards. Jonathan followed.

'Oh *no*. I'll never be that. I'm not having folk round here
poke and sneer at me or my family, specially now when all I've
aimed for is in sight, and I've a grandson into the bargain – an
heir to carry on after me—'

'An *heir*? Ask that precious wife of mine. How could he be?
I'm impotent, I tell you – *impotent*.'

Arthur threw back his head, gave another thick mocking
laugh, then stopped suddenly and faced his father with such
a look of hatred in his cold eyes and on his sneering mouth,
that Jonathan was shocked into temporary rigidity. Through
a wan beam of moonlight the younger man's raised upper
lip showed the gleam of teeth bared. So might an animal
have appeared, that had been captured and was fighting for
life.

'Arthur—' involuntarily the name slipped out. 'Calm down
now—'

But Arthur was beyond calming. From a side pocket of his
coat he brought out a revolver, pointed it waveringly at his
father and was about to press the trigger when his foot slipped,
and he fell. He scrambled to his feet then tottered backwards,
while Jonathan watched, rigid, and unmoving. There was a
splash as the body hit the surface of the water. A hand clawed
upwards, accompanied by a thin cry for help.

Arthur couldn't swim, and the pool was deep; circles of
ripples – eerily black, lit by intermittent glimmers of pale light,
widened and spread, showing briefly the greenish white coun-
tenance gasping for air.

Jonathan remained motionless, numbed of feeling, except for
a curious detached sense of relief. He made no attempt to save
his son's life, for the first time, perhaps, accepting the grim
truth that there was little, after all, worth saving.

Presently, when the last vestige of what had been Arthur
Bradley had disappeared, and the surface of the pool had
settled, Jonathan automatically picked up the revolver which

had fallen on the ground, slipped it into his pocket, turned, and made his way, on heavy feet, to the house.

No-one appeared to have heard anything. Amelia was in her bedroom at the front, with her tonic, and Emma, already asleep.

It was only the next day that Arthur's body was located — a body not only sodden with water, but with drink. The state of the horse, and other clues gave ample evidence of the manner of his end, and at the inquest later, a verdict of accidental death was reached, with due sympathy for the young widow and bereaved parents.

So Jonathan, publicly, was not involved at all.

The event in no way tarred his rising popularity, but rather evoked sympathy and respect for his fortitude in carrying on with his campaign.

Only one thing worried him. 'Impotent', Arthur had said. If that really was so . . . for days he daren't face the challenge, the terrible implication of what such a state of affairs could mean.

There was only one possible course to take.

He must ask Emma.

She wouldn't lie to him. However unsavoury her answer was, he had to know.

14

Jonathan kept silent concerning his son's last terrible taunt discrediting Emma and her baby until after the funeral. He endured the trappings of the burial service, the genuine sympathy of the countryside including many people he hardly knew, with a strong stoical set to his face, taken by all who noticed, as grief. No-one knew what he was feeling, the shocked shame mingling with a hurt so acute he could hardly accept the reality. Truth still did not completely register. At times he sensed a queer kind of Nemesis in the last disgraceful episode that had resulted in Arthur's death. He, his father, hadn't pushed him — the fates, some mysterious sense of justice, had interfered with the warped debauchery that in the end would inevitably have destroyed the bitter fruit of his, Jonathan's, union with Amelia. At other rare moments he accepted with brutal honesty that he could have saved his son, and hadn't. He'd let him die, cold-bloodedly without any attempt or wish to save him, thus sparing further disgrace — and perhaps far worse tragedy in the future. Whichever trend Jonathan's thoughts took, there was no point in debating what might or might not have been. Arthur was gone, leaving no-one really to regret him maybe, except Amelia. But the child! Emma's child — whom he'd been so fanatically proud to accept as his heir and grandson! Bitterness that could amount to hatred if Arthur's last jibe was proved to be true, gnawed to the roots of his being causing at times anguished physical pain.

At the graveside he glanced fleetingly once or twice at Emma. She appeared rigid and aloof in her black gown, her face pale, almost white behind the shroud of her veil. As far as he could tell she'd shed no tears, which was honest of her — he'd known for a considerable time that things weren't right between her and Arthur. But some slight display of emotion, he thought, might have brought a little softness to the scene. She acted befittingly in throwing a last handful of earth and a single white rose on to the coffin as it was lowered, but her actions were jerky, like those of a marionette.

She didn't preside over refreshments later in the hall and drawing room of Eastwood, but retired to her room with the plausible excuse of having a headache. None remotely guessed what she was feeling — a confused sensation of escape from a long tyranny combined with unexpected sadness over the passing of someone who'd first appeared to her as a gallant young knight come to relieve her of her many problems. She had no thought or plans for the future; her mind had become, mostly, a blank void of imagination; but beneath the cold despair a small

spark of hope, of survival, lingered. One day it must break into
flame again, whether for Evan or some other purpose there was
no knowing. The conventional answer from most people would
have been 'you have your child — your son'. This was true. At
the present time, however, the baby seemed curiously
unimportant, perhaps because of the very fact that he was
bound to bring complications to her existence ahead.

She slept heavily from exhaustion that night, and when
morning came she woke late, and had breakfast in bed before
going downstairs.

She found Jonathan waiting for her, hovering in the hall by
the library. Defying the conventional rule of wearing dead black
for a certain period following the death of a husband, she was
attired in deep purple trimmed by dark velvet braid that
emphasised subtly her delicate complexion and lustrous rich
shades of her piled up hair.

'If you'll come into the library for a moment or two, Emma,'
Jonathan said, 'I think there is a matter we must discuss. You
feel up to it, I hope?'

The directness of his question combined with the set expression and unswerving hard gleam of his eyes put her on her
guard. She drew herself up proudly and answered, 'Yes, I'm
quite all right, thank you.'

He nodded, opened the door for her, and when she'd gone
through followed her. Although the weather wasn't cold, a fire
was burning in the grate at the far end of the book-lined room.
Emma wondered, for no specific reason at all, if her father-in-
law had spent the night there. Perhaps so. Perhaps after all he'd
gone through he'd felt unable completely to relax. There was an
empty whisky bottle on a table, with a glass beside it, and a half
smoked cigar was still smouldering in a small dish among the
ash of others.

'Do sit down,' he said non-committally, and as she did so,
continued heavily, 'What I have to say isn't pleasant. If I'm
mistaken in having any doubts about — the subject, you must
accept my apologies. But—' He paused, eyeing her reflectively.

'Yes?'

He came to the point abruptly.

'Before the tragedy my son, your husband, Arthur, dropped a very nasty bombshell. He told me bluntly that he was not the father of your son. That he was impotent. Is that true, Emma?'

Her heart quickened, the tinge of colour in her cheeks drained swiftly from her face, leaving it deadly white. Her fingers tore at the shred of handkerchief in her hand as she said in faint but steady tones, 'Yes, I'm afraid so. We never − Arthur and I − never actually made love. Perhaps—'

'Then why the devil didn't you tell me?' she heard him saying harshly, so loudly that anyone listening outside must have heard. 'What do you mean by keeping a thing like that to yourself? Do you understand what you've done? Not only betrayed the family by bedding with some lusting fornicator − but withholding information I should have had so matters could have been righted. There was nothing wrong with Arthur physically. He was an athlete, a strapping man with a fine constitution. The state of affairs between you could have been *your* fault? Do you realise it − if you'd gone together to see some specialist − some − some—'

Frustration mingled with pity for the man who was so desperately trying to exonerate his son's shortcomings, at least in part, by putting the blame elsewhere caused Emma to say with more calm than she felt, 'I kept the worst things in our marriage hidden because it seemed fairer to everyone. You didn't want a scandal, did you? And that's what would have happened if I'd even tried to explain. In the end I'd have left him, because there was nothing you could have done − or I, or anyone else. Arthur was born as he was—'

'No.' Jonathan's fist was clenched. 'He was a normal baby like any other − like the one you bore, the bastard I took such pride in at first.' He was aware of a further blanching of her colour, of her lips parting, but no answering sound coming from them. 'Somewhere along the line,' he resumed heavily, 'someone − his mother, myself, you − perhaps all of us − went wrong. I notice you've not defended his statement, made no effort to excuse yourself; that being so—'

'Yes?' The word was a whisper.

'Would you mind informing me the name of the father?'

She stared at him for a moment before answering, 'I'd rather not.'

'Could it be that Welshman, Lloyd?'

She didn't reply.

The silence between them, following the last direct question was itself significant.

'I see.'

'No, you can't possibly,' Emma managed to say then. 'I've told you nothing. And I shan't — ever. For Uldene's sake. Jon's I mean.'

'Uldene. Yes. It always came first, didn't it? Your precious forest, your father, Oaklands — your — heritage.'

Her head drooped. She looked suddenly tired, drained of all energy and desire to justify herself.

He poured her a brandy and handed it to her.

'Drink it up. Now the inquisition's over I'll tell you what I mean to do.'

'*You?*'

'The boy was born a Bradley. And a Bradley he'll remain. Concerning his background you'll hold your tongue, for the sake of us all, especially his. To the outside world he'll be my grandson and heir, and by God his bringing up will be different from Arthur's. No molly-coddling by that stupid wife of mine, no public school where drink and sodomy get a grip before a lad's character's properly formed. He'll have an understanding but strict tutor here — or perhaps Rugby. I've heard there are no twisted goings on there. Whatever I choose for him he'll get, and grin and bear it like a gentleman. Do you understand, Emma? I'll shape him somehow into the son I always wanted—?' He broke off, breathing heavily.

When Emma spoke it was drily, but with an undercurrent of temper rising in her. 'And what about me?'

'You? Things will go on here as they began. But the Dower House will be out. You won't need it now.'

'And I may not need *you*.' Before she knew it the statement was out.

His complexion turned a deep red. 'What do you mean? What are you implying?'

'I'm his mother. He's *my* child, I bore him. No-one's going to say what he does and does not do, or what his education will be, but me — *me*. You understand?' Her eyes flashed, changing from grey to blue-green lit by flecks of dancing gold. Temper made her suddenly not only beautiful but irresistible. Determination mingled with a strange sense of defeat and desire rose in Jonathan's breast driving him towards her. A hand touched a soft shoulder, lingered there, then fell to his side with fingers digging into his palms. Both were breathing quickly — she, because she sensed the conflict in him, he through thwarted emotions. 'If thing's were otherwise,' she heard him say, 'if you were not my daughter-in-law, I'd sire a son by you myself.' He turned away. 'Arthur was not only a disgrace, but a fool.'

'He was mad, Jonathan.'

He turned to look at her again. 'Is that all you can say?'

'There's nothing more *to* say, is there? You've made your intentions perfectly clear, and you know mine.'

'No, I *don't*. I want confirmation — your promise, that you'll agree to my plans for the boy. You're a woman of your word, as much as any human being *can* be. I give you credit for that.' He paused, 'Well?'

Sympthy for him, a sudden awareness of how deep his hurt was, combined with an acceptance of her own position and the child's, that she was beginning to believe Evan might never see, softened her sufficiently to ambiguous agreement. 'I'll — keep things to myself,' she said, 'and stay here, as long as it seems right, and works out. I don't want to harm Arthur's image more than necessary—'

'He's done that himself already,' Jonathan interrupted harshly. 'Only the boy matters now. You understand?' He thumped his chest hard. 'In time maybe I'll manage to forget or lay aside just as a bad memory, the way he came into being. But you must stand by me, so the word bastard never fouls the Bradley name.'

She remained silent.

Before the interlude between them ended, he said, 'I rely on you never to divulge a word of this to my wife. Women like Amelia are inclined to let their tongues wag under certain — stimulus. And Jessie.'

'I shouldn't dream of confiding in either,' Emma remarked rather coldly, thinking wrily that it was quite conceivable both had a good idea of the truth.

'Hm.'

As Jonathan walked to the door opening it for her to leave, she noticed that he appeared to have aged ten years. The next day, however, his energy and spirits seemed to have revived. He had a heavy day of canvassing and returned late to Eastwood fanatically determined to win in the forthcoming election. 'With Wendle behind me, and the constituency well primed,' he said, 'I don't see I can lose.'

His prophecy proved to be correct. In January 1906, Jonathan Bradley was elected as MP to Westminster.

For his sake, Emma was pleased. She had to be, living at East-wood, and with still no word of Evan.

Evan!

Every time his image unwillingly invaded her mind, she thrust it ruthlessly away, believing she would probably never see him again.

15

Almost from his earliest days, the tiny Jon Uldene displayed an increasing interest in Jonathan. Bradley, so busy most days either in his constituency, or on frequent visits to Westminster where he made an effective maiden speech, did not at first spend much time with the child. Emma and the nursemaid had full command in the nursery; besides, apart from his fresh resonsibilities, there were still board meetings of the *Comet* and proposed *Midlander* to attend to. However, during the first days of early spring, something about the small entity destined to play such a vital part in his life, stirred a gradually awakening response. He couldn't help being aware of the child's large greyish blue eyes following him solemnly when he left the room after a brief visit to the nursery, or of the clinging of tiny fingers to his hand whenever he gave a pat to a plump cheek or dig to the stomach. Such gestures were intended primarily as an indication to Emma that he bore Jon no resentment, only goodwill. But inevitably the baby's curiosity, and obvious pleasure in his company, woke a grudging affection which had nothing to do with the fact that Jon Uldene was merely a substitute for the real grandson he'd hoped for. What did genes matter, after all? They were important, of course; nothing could alter the fact that his heir hadn't been sired a Bradley by blood. But there was something else — closeness, an affinity of spirit, which could, given a chance, mean more. And miraculously this quality had been inbued somehow between man and infant from the very beginning of the little boy's birth.

On Jon, beyond all Jonathan's aspirations for the future, both politically and in business, his hopes became more firmly fixed. A latent sense of humour developed between them. A comical face or wiggling of a finger, a strange attitude when Bradley pretended to be a dog begging and barking — brought gurgles of delight from the baby. On such occasions the man himself felt gratified and amused, though such antics only happend in Emma's absence — he'd already sensed a rising unacknowledged jealousy in her which he didn't wish to provoke.

Once, when the nursemaid was in the bathroom, and the baby alone in his cot cooing softly, Amelia came to the door quietly and heard her husband say as he bent down, 'Eh, well, son, you're one of us all right. Jonathan *Bradley*, and don't you forget it.' There was a pause before he added, 'My *grandson*,' with a kind of wonder in his voice.

An inadvertent slight cough from Amelia jerked him up abruptly. Turning, he saw her standing there, appearing mildly embarrassed and ashamed.

'Sorry,' she muttered apologetically. 'I wasn't prying, Jonathan, I was coming along to see the little one myself.'

After his first stab of annoyance her husband cleared his throat, covered his irritation, and said, 'Eh, well! come along in then. You've as much right as anyone, I reckon, to have a peep now and then. But don't go spoiling him, Amelia, not like you did — Arthur. No sweetmeats out of mealtimes or mollycoddling and cuddling when you get the chance. This one's going to be a real man when he grows up. One to do us credit.'

'Aye, you're right,' Amelia said, glowing with pleasure to hear once more the warm North Country accent in her husband's voice.

It was perhaps unfortunate that at such a moment Emma should appear upon the scene. She was looking particularly lovely in a dress of primrose yellow that gave a golden glow to her skin, enriching the piled-up copper glint of her rich hair.

A stab of jealousy seized her. Although she smiled, her voice was brittle when she asked, 'Where's Lily, his nurse?'

'Getting a fresh nappy, I wouldn't wonder,' Amelia answered quickly, sniffing comically. 'You need it, don't you, ducks?' she reached down and took the baby up into her plump arms. Emma instantly pulled Jon from her.

Jonathan gave a grunt. 'We're not wanted here obviously,' he said. 'Come along, Amelia, leave him to his mother.'

They had turned to leave when the baby started to wail, kicking his tiny knees at Emma's stomach. Amelia went out, but Jonathan stood briefly at the door before returning to the cot where mother and child were standing.

At the sight of his face the little boy's temper died. He quietened, staring at Bradley for a full few seconds before a slow smile spread from ear to ear.

'Now then, you just be good,' Jonathan said. 'No fireworks, understand. Be nice to your mama now and behave—'

His eyes sought Emma's, half pleadingly. 'It's always the same with babies.' His voice was gruff, placating. 'Never know what they want from one moment to the next. It was the same with—' he was about to say 'Arthur', but withheld it in time, and said, 'Jessie.'

'I know,' Emma retorted lightly. 'And I should be used to my own child's moods by now.' But she wasn't. There were occasions when she found herself completely bewildered, even irritated by her son's unpredictable behaviour. He was hers — hers and Evan's. Then why did he have to show such obvious preference for Jonathan's company? Perhaps he was becoming too much immersed in the atmosphere of Eastwood. After all, by blood he was a Fairley. The time had come, quite clearly, when he should have more contact with Burnwood and Oaklands.

In the April of that year 1906, she was once more able to take an active interest in the weekly publication of *Woman's Post*, and decided that in future she would take Jon with her on fine days, leaving him in the charge of Mrs Cox at Oaklands during her sessions at Charbrook for board meetings or on editorial business.

Mrs Cox was pleased to have him; with her he was good, although distinctly unresponsive. Rosalind tried, in her simple way, to be friendly, but it was as though Jon sensed something 'different' about her; he would stare at her from his huge eyes, with his thumb in his mouth, as though already assessing her personality. Being a forward child for his age, he could already say intelligible words, some of which he'd concocted himself. Animals delighted him.

Once, feeling particularly generous Rosalind offered him her favourite teddy bear to hold. He pushed it away contemptuously, and would not even have it in his push-cart. Rosalind had one of her tempers, ending in a fit of screaming. Emma, after comforting her with a gift — a box of candies she'd brought — carried the baby to one of her favourite spots from where the ruined priory could be seen swathed in a thin veil of silvery mist, and in the other direction the glint of deep blue-green through the trees. Far beyond the woods, the rocky tips of Hawkshill rose above the ancient granite hamlet of Eavesley.

'One day,' Emma said, lifting the child as high as she could, in her arms, 'I'll take you up there; the rocks are like tiny castles, and rabbits have their homes there. There are all kinds of things to find — and secret places where you can hide—' Her words trailed off dreamily. She knew he wasn't listening, and if he did, he wouldn't understand. But the quiet magic of the forest was all about her.

When the soft wind brushed a cheek it was as though whispers from the past stirred old memories to life again; she was a child, immersed in a world of ancient legendry in which every stirring of the grass, or a branch shaking its leaves, was indicative of some stranger's approach — a presence unseen — exciting and mysterious, who could be anyone or anything, gnarled witch, or handsome knight taking shape from the shadows. As puberty approached fairy-tales had somehow merged into reality, but the reality was no less magical, holding the wonder of growing things and murmur of brooks rippling over the stones; of the sweet damp earth pulsing with life in the spring — tips of bluebells and curling golden-green ferns, lush clearings and dells starred with celandines, violets, and golden heads of kingcups by marshy ground. And on the verge of the forest, fields and fields of buttercups!

So beautiful! So far removed from the pain that life could bring.

As she stared that day through the interlaced branches of the at the shimmering sky, the inevitable picture returned of the time she'd first lain with Evan in the grass.

Would she ever see him again? Would Jon ever know his father? Would he realise when he was older, one small fraction of what this place meant to her?

She put him down gently, to relieve her aching arms. He started to grumble instantly. Bending down and staring into his eyes, she said, 'Isn't it nice here, then? Don't you like it, Jon?'

Obviously he didn't. Disappointment filled her. He was still only a baby, of course, but surely something in the vicinity of Oaklands must strike a chord somewhere in his being – an inborn sense of familiarity bred through William and his fore-fathers.

No. She had to accept that he was wanting Eastwood, and probably Jonathan.

Jonathan!

A fit of irritation swept through her. 'Oh, come along then,' she said, 'We'll get back. I won't go to Charbrook today. You've tired me out already.'

Following this visit she made others with her young son. Sometimes he displayed an interest at the sight of some shy deer or lolloping rabbit, but mostly he appeared bored or fractious. Her will asserted itself then; she became firmer, even at times quick-tempered, having to accept that Jonathan was his idol, and would have to be stopped spoiling him and giving the little boy so much attention.

The idea occurred to her of moving for a time to Oaklands, in this way forcing the child to accept his true environment. She broached the suggestion tentatively to Amelia.

'Oh I wouldn't, love,' her mother-in-law advised, shaking her head. 'You know how it is – Jonathan's set his heart on thinking the boy's his own—'

'Yes. That's the trouble. He *isn't*. He's mine.'

'But after all he went through, with Arthur, wouldn't it be kind of – cruel – to separate them?'

'It would only be for periods.'

'Would it, love?' Amelia sounded unconvinced.

Emma didn't reply.

After this short conversation life went on for a time in its usual way, except that *Woman's Post* once more assumed greater importance in Emma's life. She started an advice column on social and domestic problems which at the beginning brought in only a few letters — occasionally from male readers of a sarcastic nature. One even ended by saying '. . . first let Lady Anne—' the name she wrote under 'learn her onions, and grow up a bit before trotting out clichés to wives and grandmothers. Or maybe she writes and answers those rubbishy notes herself?'.

Emma's face flamed when she read it, because for the first two issues she *had* had to resort to such devious means in three cases. Her first reaction was to end the new feature, then decided to battle on with it, and answered by writing:

> If the gentleman concerned, and I must assume he *is* a gentleman — refrained from interfering with two columns headed 'FOR WOMEN ONLY' he would not find himself in the humiliating position of professing such ignorance of feminine affairs. I notice he gives no address or legitimate name — only a non-de-plume. However, if he wishes further education concerning home-making and marriage, I can assure him Lady Anne will do her utmost to help.

Following this exchange, correspondence between readers and the editorial department, speeded up, and the recently appointed new managing editor of the combined *Echo* and *Woman's Post* congratulated Emma on her titillating brainchild.

Apart from this mainly light side of the paper, Emma still found time to write a monthly article on some serious topic such as housing and health. There was always a short space in the magazine for 'Gardening Tips', and one for 'Creative Crafts', dealt with by the girl journalist. Fashion — except for 'Home Dressmaking' was not included. The magazine did not attempt to present a glamorous image. In catering for the ordinary girl, wife, and mother, both in country and town districts, it earned an increasingly appreciative public.

And yet, Emma thought once or twice, as she drove back to Eastwood, what right, really, had *she* to give any hints on marriage-making, especially when her own had been so abnormal? Would her father have admired and congratulated her on her venture which had enabled the *Echo* to continue for considerably longer than Bradley otherwise would have allowed it to? Also the Fairley name was still known in the newspaper world, even though in a different sphere than William had anticipated. She had moved with the times, that was all. But there was nothing brash or garish about her contribution. *Woman's Post* was a healthy thriving shoot sprung from her father's dream. In this way she had justified her inheritance. Everyone 'in the know', of course, realised that the *Echo* was very gradually being faded out into The *Midlander*. Jonathan was chagrined that he had not also been able to acquire the *Courier*. But so far he was having to accept that the older well-established Leyford daily was far too firmly rooted in traditional appeal, and too well trusted to be shaken by any new company, however large and powerful. One thing, he discovered, somewhat to his surprise, money could *not* buy – and that was loyalty.

He meant to go on trying, but was doubtful by then of any fruitful outcome. The *Midlander* might prove a worthy rival, and more successful than the *Comet*, but the *Courier*, independent, non-political, sound and trustworthy in its views, had already proved unshakable through the county and elsewhere. Jonathan, having acquired his seat in Westminster, no longer fretted over losing this certain newspaper battle. The other papers were thriving, and he had an honest respect for any privately owned company that could squarely face a formidable challenge and win.

He had, as well, this further growing interest in his life – young Jon. Sometimes, in the rare leisure moments when he'd been playing with the child, a dull sense of dread filled him at the thought a day might come when Emma might want to marry again, and take him from the family to another home. Would she have the right to uproot him in such an event? Or could he, as legal grandfather, have a claim? Knowing the former was probably true, that he'd fight if he had to, but probably fail, he was careful to please his daughter-in-law by all means in his power, fanning and intensifying her interest and involvement with *Woman's Post* so she felt secure and unhampered in her life at Eastwood.

One day, in early September when Emma was feeling irritated by a fractious interlude with her young son, she drove herself, in a fit of nostalgia, towards Oaklands, not Charbrook or on any journalistic business, but solely to be alone in her own environment of the forest. Autumn, to her, was always a nostalgic period, and the woods at their most colourful. The morning was fine, clear and golden, faintly filmed by thin blueish mist hovering about hill, lanes and hedgerows. There was no wind, no stirring through foliage or undergrowth, although occasionally a brown leaf floated down from a tree as she passed. She took the drive leisurely, steering down any particular lane that took her fancy. Before reaching the more thickly wooded areas, she had a sudden urge to see the park, and made a detour to Bradgate. She stopped the car at the gates, parked it and entered the old historical territory.

Not far from the main drive the brook rippled between rocks and over stones shot with gold and silver light from the climbing sun. The white tails of rabbits bobbed in the tall bracken — russet and brown now — as she passed. A deer, soft-eyed, stood for a moment watching under an ancient oak, then moved gracefully up the slope towards a thicket of trees. Emma glanced upwards. Staring down, quite motionless, was the proud antlered shape of a red stag.

She'd been warned time after time when she was young, never to approach a male deer near the rutting season, but had taken little advice. Neither did she now. From being a young child she'd felt an affinity with all creatures of the forest, and that day was no exception. At one point the richly shaded satin-coated form came a few yards nearer, then leisurely turned and with arched neck, proud head raised magnificently, retreated into the shadowed copse.

Emma continued her walk, taking the turn by the ruined

mansion which had once been the home of the unfortunate Lady Jane Grey, and then, suddenly — coming towards her down a slope on her left, she saw him; a sturdy youngish figure, bare-headed, with the morning light touching his brown hair to gold.

Evan.

It was like a dream coming to life. So many times during the past year she'd envisioned him, in sleep, somehow, somewhere — appearing unexpectedly — round a corner of a road, at the top of a flight of stairs, or at the end of a long corridor — on a mountain side, or in a crowded thoroughfare or dance hall — but always out of reach. In her sleep she'd called to him and run struggling to catch him before he vanished. But he'd always gone — sometimes merely fading, as though forces beyond her control pulled him, at others he'd himself shaken his head and left her, becoming no more than a shadow in all the other shadows of that unseen twilight world.

When she'd woken there'd generally been tears on her lashes, with a terrible sense of loss in her heart.

But now! *now* — she stood for a second or two staring; he did the same. And then suddenly they were running towards each other, and she was locked in an embrace so hard, so wild and filled with joy they couldn't at first speak.

How long they remained silent they never knew. The world was hushed and filled with wonder about them.

Evan was back. He had come home — to her, and the forest.

16

After that first passionate reunion, they walked hand in hand through the golden afternoon to where Emma's car was parked. They got in, and Evan's arm once more went round her, drawing her closer. He had been to Eastwood apparently, and having been told 'Mrs Arthur' was out, by a maid, and that no-one knew when she'd be back, he'd guessed and hoped he might find her at Oaklands, and had driven there in his own small car.

The housekeeper had informed him when he arrived she wasn't expected that day. In a desultory way he'd wandered around for some time, wondering whether or not to go on to Charbrook, and then, suddenly he'd had the idea of walking through the park.

'Must have been a sixth sense — telepathy, if you like,' he told her. 'Oh Emma, my sweet, wild, wilful love — why didn't you answer my letters?'

'Letters? But I never had one — not from Africa,' she told him, only one from Ireland. Arthur must have—'

'That swine! If I could get my hands on him I'd—' Lloyd explained.

'You can't,' Emma stated in such flat dulled tones he glanced at her sharply. 'No-one can. Arthur's dead.'

'Oh. That means—?'

'Yes,' she said before he could finish, 'I'm free, and yet I'm not — in a way. I'm bound, just as much as you are, Evan — but differently.'

'What do you mean?'

Haltingly at first, then in a rush, the words came tumbling out. The whole story of her discovery that she was having a baby — *his* child — of the long endless months of waiting to hear from him, of longing, despair, Jon's birth and Arthur's tragic death, followed by her determination to survive and her fanatical dedication to *Woman's Post*.

'It was like being a machine,' she said at last. 'I just went on and on—'

'But why the devil didn't you let me know about the baby?' Evan demanded, 'It was my right, and presumably you knew the last time we met, in London?'

'Oh yes. But before I could say, you callously informed me you had a wife,' Emma retorted sharply. 'How do you think I felt then? But perhaps you *didn't* think at all. Perhaps you assumed I was just content to be an incident—' Renewed indignation flooded her voice and lovely eyes.

He took both her shoulders and forced her round to face him. 'Now look here, my love, none of that; don't you *dare* suggest such a thing. A bare-faced lie, and you know it. And if you go on in this way I'll – I'll—'

'Yes, Evan?' Her tones were suddenly meek.

'I'll put you over my knee and wallop you soundly in public. Damned if I won't.'

'How interesting for the birds and bees and baby rabbits,' she said, with no trace of expression on her face. He relaxed, smiling slightly, then said more quietly, 'Don't joke, Emma.'

'I'm not. It's just – oh so much has happened, and now you suddenly appear and I'm sort of lost and quite out of my depth. Because you see, nothing's solved really. There's still Shirin; and Jon, my little boy – he's like you, Evan, but it's his grandfather who matters to him. I don't really see any possibility of us being together.'

'Then you'd better start looking,' Evan replied brusquely. 'Because I'm not letting you off the chain any more, my love, and I want my son. You'd better get that into your head once and for all.'

'How can I? And what would I be to you? A sort of permanent mistress during the time you're not in Ireland?'

He gritted his teeth, and staring stonily ahead, through the wind-screen, said, 'I shall never go to Ireland again.'

'But, Shirin—'

'Shirin also is dead.'

'Oh.'

'It happened months ago. She had a kind of seizure, a fit. It wasn't pleasant. I happened to be there at the time, and I'm glad now. Her aunt needed someone, and even a womanising kind of adventurer like me can have feelings, a sense of duty if you like.'

There was a pause, followed by Emma saying, 'Oh Evan, I'm sorry.'

'No need to be. Poor Shirin's well out of it. You regretted your father's death – that was natural. He happened to be a normal human being. But I've no patience with anyone pretending to moan at the end of a crazy unhappy creature's suffering, whether a human being or animal. So please let us drop the subject.'

'Of course,' she agreed quietly, feeling rebuked for her own insensitivity. Of *course* Evan was hurt, and still remembered the past, as she did her own – with Arthur. However impossible and unfortunate both she and Evan's marriages had been, they'd *happened*, and helped make each of them the people they now were – able to understand better, and add a wider dimension to their own loving.

She let her fingers stray lightly over Evan's near hand. 'There's a lot we'll have to put aside now,' she said, 'and accept about each other.'

'Yes,' said Evan. 'It's the future we have to think about.'

Which they proceeded to do, without any further delay.

*

Emma at first was all in favour that she and Evan should be married before informing the Bradleys, Jonathan in particular. But Evan was determined to have everything in the open. 'There's been too much secrecy already,' he told her the next day when they met in Leyford, 'too many devious undercurrents and evasions. Bradley won't like it, of course, but he's got other fish to fry now, with all his Parliamentary commitments. When we're off the scene with young Jon he'll adapt and come round in the end and see sense. Jon's *my* son, after all. And anyway I suppose we'll keep in touch—'

'Oh Evan — *keep in touch*!' Emma shook her head. 'You don't understand one half of what the baby means to that man. They're *devoted*. It's as though—'

'What?'

'As though—' Emma broke off, searching for words, then continued hesitantly, '—as though it was *meant*.'

'What do you mean *meant*?'

'For Jon to take Arthur's place,' she said bluntly.

'But—'

'*No*. Wait. Just listen to me first and then say what you like. I know you've got a point in wanting to claim Jon. But he doesn't know you — he's never even *seen* you. All these months, more than a year, when I never had a line from you and made myself plan my future round the *Woman's Post*, *driving* myself, doing my damnedest to forget you, Jonathan and Jon have forged a bond—'

'Forged a *bond*! Come now, Emma. This is real life. How can a baby forge anything?'

'Wait until you see our son,' she said calmly, almost grimly, 'then you'll get a surprise.'

There was a long pause before Evan queried stiffly, 'Are you trying to suggest that we start our married life without the child?'

Her clear grey eyes stared directly into his. She shook her head slowly.

'No, darling. I'm not suggesting anything yet. But it's a possibility, isn't it? And would it be so bad, just you and I together?'

Gazing at her, entranced utterly once more by the pale heart-shaped face framed by its wayward wealth of dark russet curls — by the tilted trembling mouth and arch of slim neck, above all by her honesty and sincerity which still held so much of a child's innocence, he knew that indeed *with* her he would have everything, and without her nothing.

The well-remembered whimsical smile touched his mouth.

'You *are* a superb actress, Emma,' he murmured, before his lips enclosed hers.

'*Actress?* How dare you?'

'Oh I dare, my darling. Never doubt my courage. And you won't always win, you know, in any battle ahead of us.'

'I wouldn't want to, Evan Lloyd. Just so long as you promise one thing.'

'What?'

'Not to go jaunting off to foreign climes leaving me at Oaklands alone ever again.

'That's a bargain. But neither do I intend being tied to your apron strings. More likely you'll have a halter round your neck. And then Oaklands! – you seem to have arranged things pretty quickly in your nimble mind. Who said we were going to live there?'

'Me. For part of the time anyway.'

'I'm glad you added the last bit. Because there's another world beyond, you know, *my* land. Oh, *cariad*, my sweet wild Emma, one day I'll take you there. There's music in the valleys, and the mountains have a mystery and magic about them you find nowhere else. There's poverty too, and bigotry in parts, but hearts are warm and generous. Until we go there together, I can't properly explain. How can I?' He smiled again whimsically, 'A Welshman treading the soil of England!'

'Now you're Evan Lloyd the poet,' Emma remarked, 'and I know – I've *always* known – that the public will accept you one day.'

'Public be damned,' Evan said vigorously, 'haven't I got all I want right here in my arms?'

'Yes – oh yes,' she agreed, 'and so have I. But your work matters, your own particular kind of talent, your unique sort of Welshness, and that's going to be our aim – *mine* anyway – to spread it everywhere, around the world.'

They were both being ridiculously exultantly confident, and were well aware of it. But it didn't matter. Nothing was of any account at the moment beyond their coming together again.

Later, when the practical point arose of informing Jonathan

of their plants and intended marriage, Jonathan was at first assessingly doubtful, then grudgingly acquiescent.

'If you want to do such a mad-headed thing,' he told his daughter-in-law grimly, 'you'll do it. I should know you by now. But the boy!' He thrust his jaw out before enquiring bluntly, 'I take it you'll leave him here where he rightly belongs? Legally he was born my grandson, and I think I can give him greater security and personal contentment than you two ever will—'

Evan's temper flared.

'You've no right to say that. A son's place is with his parents. I happen to be his father, and I think the law would agree—'

'The law has nothing to do with it. If it came to a battle in court your own claim would be nullified immediately. As for Emma—' His voice softened slightly. 'I think if she's honest — which she generally is — she'll agree with me that the youngster's happier here than at Oaklands. Another thing — there'll most likely soon be other children coming along, once you're wed. Well — think about it. There's plenty of time. Get to know the boy a bit. When you see how things are, I reckon you'll agree what I've said is right.'

This proved to be true. Although Evan recognised and was proud of Jon's looks, healthy stamina, and bright mind — no true affinity registered between them. To all intents and purposes the toddler had been born and destined to become a Bradley.

So it was settled, not without certain heart-searching on Emma's part.

On a day in late October 1906, Mrs Arthur Bradley became Mrs Evan Lloyd, and the one true adventure of their joint life began.

A son was born the following year, followed by twins in 1910. By then King Edward VII had died, and a new monarch was on the throne. 'The *Echo* had successfully been amalgamated with the *Comet* into The *Midlander*, but *Woman's Post* thrived and at the time of the Coronation a special edition was published showing photographs of the event.

So began a dynasty of magazine enterprise first founded by

the Fairley family, which eventually had a counterpart in America.

But that is another story.

Emma and Evan had the normal difficulties, successes, arguments and makings up of any passionate couple deeply in love.

Meanwhile the life of the forest went on, unchanged except for a few tourists in summer time.

William's faith in Emma was justified.

Oaklands was safe, for all time.

EPILOGUE

1915

On a cold day in nineteen fifteen, Emma Lloyd and her three children stood on a platform at Leyford Station watching the train puff in that was to take Evan to the Front. It was wartime. Countless other women and their families waited with her as Evan, only one of the khaki-clad crowd, was jostled through a door into the maze of steamy corridors and compartments.

Thin sleet, mingled with smoke, half obscured the features of loved faces pressed against windows eagerly searching for a last glance of the ones to be left behind.

Emma, for the sake of the children, tried to appear controlled. But her eyes were half blinded with tears, as following a parting embrace, her husband shouted, 'Thumbs up, Emma *cariad*, I'll be back.'

The next moment the slow throbbing of the train's engine increased, taking the serpent-like shape gradually into a blurred distance of thickening nonentity. The desperate waving of handkerchiefs and disc-like watching faces finally disappeared.

It was over.

For many, the last farewells had been said, to leave a blankness and emptiness in hearts which could never completely be filled again.

Presently, one by one, and then in small groups, the families turned, and moved slowly from the platform. As Emma, grasping the hands of the twins, accompanied by her elder son, William, passed up the steps to the station entrance, she noticed a poster depicting Kitchener with a pointing finger, and a message printed bodly by it, saying 'Your Country Needs You'. Further on there was another — 'Make the Cap Fit. *WEAR IT*.'

As the four of them entered the sleet-blown street, she heard above the rattle of tram-cars the voices of girls singing from a nearby pub:

> Oh we don't want to lose you, but we think you ought
>   to go —
> For your King and your Country, *do* need you so.
> We shall love you and miss you, but with all our
>   might and main,
> We will hug you, thank you, kiss you —
> When you come back again —

Would Evan come back? *Would* he? But of course. He *must*. He'd promised. Clinging to the hope, she walked on courageously, while one tiny voice asked, 'Will it take Daddy long to win the war, Mummy?'

'No. Not long, darling,' Emma answered, hoping and praying desperately that it would be true, but that even if he didn't, the new world those thousands of young men were fighting and dying for, would be worthwhile.